"You Know What Your Problem Is, Alec?" Daisy Demanded. "You Don't Trust Anybody."

"Of course I trust people," Alec answered quickly.

"Liar. And your suspicious nature ruined my plan for tonight."

"You had a plan?"

"Yes, I did, and no thanks to you...." She tipped her head to one side, considering Alec with an expression that made him uneasy.

As he waited for her to come clean with her big plan he tried not to notice the way she tugged at her lower lip with her teeth.

"Ah, what the hell," Daisy said, taking a step closer. "I'm going to Plan B."

And with that, she went up on her toes, placed her fingertips on his shoulders and gently touched her warm lips to his.

Dear Reader,

Welcome to another passionate month at Silhouette Desire where the menu is set with another fabulous title in our DYNASTIES: THE DANFORTHS series. Linda Conrad provides *The Laws of Passion* when Danforth heir Marc must clear his name or face the consequences. And here's a little something to whet your appetite—the second installment of Annette Broadrick's THE CRENSHAWS OF TEXAS. What's a man to do when he's *Caught in the Crossfire*— actually, when he's caught in bed with a senator's daughter? You'll have to wait and see....

Our mouthwatering MANTALK promotion continues with Maureen Child's *Lost in Sensation*. This story, entirely from the hero's point of view, will give you insight into a delectable male—what fun! Kristi Gold dishes up a tasty tidbit with *Daring the Dynamic Sheikh*, the concluding title in her series THE ROYAL WAGER. Rochelle Alers's series THE BLACKSTONES OF VIRGINIA is back with *Very Private Duty* and a hunk you can dig right into. And be sure to save room for the delightful treat that is Julie Hogan's *Business or Pleasure?*

Here's hoping that this month's Silhouette Desire selections will fulfill your craving for the best in sensual romance... and leave you hungry for more!

Happy devouring!

Melissa Jeglinski

Melissa Jeglinski
Senior Editor
Silhouette Desire

Please address questions and book requests to:
Silhouette Reader Service
U.S.: 3010 Walden Ave., P.O. Box 1325, Buffalo, NY 14269
Canadian: P.O. Box 609, Fort Erie, Ont. L2A 5X3

BUSINESS OR *Pleasure?*

JULIE HOGAN

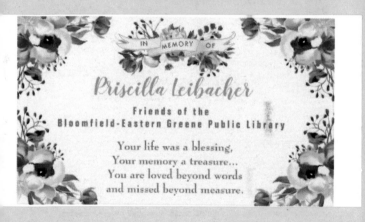

Silhouette® *Desire*

Published by Silhouette Books
America's Publisher of Contemporary Romance

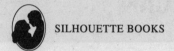

SILHOUETTE BOOKS

ISBN 0-373-76614-9

BUSINESS OR PLEASURE?

Copyright © 2004 by Julie Hogan

Visit Silhouette Books at www.eHarlequin.com

Printed in U.S.A.

Books by Julie Hogan

Silhouette Desire

Tangled Sheets, Tangled Lies #1500
Business or Pleasure? #1614

JULIE HOGAN

discovered romance novels at the age of ten and spent her youthful summers tearing through one book after another when she should have been doing chores at her parents' northern San Diego County avocado orchard. Luckily, in spite of a checkered past that ranged from undercover department store security to "hotwalking" thoroughbred horses at the Santa Anita racetrack, all that summer reading paid off. After ten years in the rat race, Julie gave up her career as an internet marketing executive and, with her English degree from UCLA clutched in her fist, finally realized her dream of writing her own romance novels. Julie shares a quiet, Southern California home with her true-to-life hero husband, Jud, who inspires both her writing and her life, and two bad-tempered cats who rule the neighborhood with an iron claw. In her writing, Julie enjoys bringing funny and engaging characters to life, then putting them through the wringer until they realize that love is the only true path to happiness. The only thing Julie loves more than reading and writing romances is hearing from readers who share her mania. You can write to her at julie@juliehogan.com.

To David Ankrum, who stands in my corner and encourages me, nudges me and makes me laugh.

To Stephanie Maurer, the very soul of patience, supportiveness and genuine niceness.

And to my husband and my son, who make my life a heaven on earth.

One

"**M**ackenzie, you are the luckiest damned guy in the world," Todd Herly said as he hefted his golf bag onto his shoulder.

Alec Mackenzie hid a smile. "I'm going to tell your wife you're cussing again."

"Go ahead," his friend snapped as they walked toward the Riviera Country Club's parking lot, their cleats clicking rhythmically on the concrete path. "When the kids aren't around, I can do whatever I want."

Alec laughed, shifting his own clubs higher on his shoulder. "Sure you can, buddy."

"Anyway, that's not what we're talking about. We're talking about how scoring the Santa Margarita contract makes you the luckiest man alive."

"Luck had nothing to do with it. I won this contract fair

and square. I worked for this," he said, indicating the thick manila envelope in his hand, "which is more than I can say for you and your company, which, as usual, threw together an inflated proposal that probably didn't even make it onto the client's radar."

Todd, the man who was both his best friend and his most ardent and talented professional rival, gasped in predictable outrage.

Alec just grinned. "Of course," he said, "when it came down to the wire, my charm, charisma and good looks probably helped clinch the deal."

"I doubt it," Todd shot back. "Although, I'm sure that's what you used to get that tall, cool drink of water to hand over her phone number at the benefit Saturday night."

"Jealous?" Alec joked as they approached their cars.

"Hardly. Chelle would eat me alive if she even suspected that I'd looked twice at a woman that gorgeous."

"Chelle *is* that gorgeous," Alec said and meant it. Todd and his wife were perfect for each other, a regular storybook romance. But Alec was a man who liked his freedom, and he meant to keep it that way. Not that his bachelor status was in jeopardy. Far from it. In fact, the woman he'd met the other night was going to be just the ticket for a few weeks of fun. She was beautiful, had legs up to here and…well, that pretty much made her ideal.

Alec slipped his prized clubs into the passenger seat of his convertible Ferrari Spider and turned to his oldest friend. "I better get going. I've got to get this," he said, tapping a teasing finger on the envelope, "to the office."

Todd frowned as he slammed the trunk of the big Mercedes he'd recently bought because—as he'd sheepishly explained to Alec—it was the perfect sedan for his family of four. "I take it back, Mackenzie," Todd said. "You're not the luckiest man alive, you're the most competitive. You always have been."

Alec climbed into the fastest sports car on the market and slid the contract that named his firm the victor in a protracted battle for the most coveted architectural redesign project in southern California into the glove compartment. "Winning is what matters, Todd," he said as he fired up the engine and threw the car into reverse. "The *only* thing that matters."

Todd opened his mouth to protest, but Alec just waved and sped away with *The Eagles' Greatest Hits* pouring out of the stereo's speakers.

By the time the band had launched into the opening notes of "Desperado," Alec was halfway to his Santa Monica office. It doesn't get any better than this, he thought as he sped down a winding, tree-shaded patch of Sunset Boulevard and hummed along with the old tune. Breakfast at the country club with his best friend and a solid hour at the driving range would have been enough to make for a great morning. But the arrival of a messenger from the office bearing the news that his firm had won the project had been the best possible interruption.

He pulled into a parking space under his company's building and opened the glove compartment. Todd was right. Alec had a lucky streak in him a mile wide—and a competitive one at least a mile and a half wide. But this, he thought as he grabbed the contract, he deserved.

Alec wasn't shy about his abilities as an architect so he'd only been half kidding when he'd told Todd that his talent had won the contract. He was, he thought as he stepped inside the waiting elevator and punched the button for the top floor, very good at what he did. And he and his team had put together an extremely competitive bid.

But now that the contract was in his hands, he realized that in spite of his confidence—some would say ego—he still couldn't quite believe it. Just off the southern California coast on the tiny island of Santa Margarita, seven historical but decaying mansions were going to be restored to their former glory and reopened as five-star bed and breakfasts. And he and his company were going to do the job.

"Mackenzie Architectural Revivals," he heard his receptionist say into the phone as she looked up and smiled. "How may I direct your call?"

He winked at her and headed for his office. Yessir, this was shaping up to be one hell of a day.

His assistant, Daisy Kincaid, wasn't at her desk when he walked by, but he only had to take one step into his office to see she'd already been there. Neatly arranged on his prized Frank Lloyd Wright desk were all of life's little essentials: a cup of hot coffee, a couple of his favorite Krispy Kremes, the day's *Los Angeles Times* and a stack of trade magazines.

He sat down, propped his feet up on the desk, put his head back and smiled, really smiled, for the first time in weeks.

"Did you get it?"

Alec looked up and saw Daisy leaning against the door frame. She, too, wore a wide, delighted smile, and for a second, just one second, he saw something he'd never seen before. She looked almost…pretty.

The jacket of her tailored gray jacket was unbuttoned, showing a flash of soft, smoky colored T-shirt beneath, her dark-brown eyes danced happily behind her wire-framed glasses, and curly strands of her chestnut hair had escaped her perpetual twist, suddenly making him feel like he wanted to pull out the pins one by one.

He shook his head to scatter the image. A trick of the light, he thought, or maybe just another sign that today was magical because during the three years she'd worked for him, he'd never once been tempted to use the word pretty to describe Daisy. *Loyal, hardworking, efficient, smart, resourceful, responsible*—those were the words he would use. Nope, she wasn't pretty, but for what she did so well here at his company, she was exactly what he needed.

He swung his legs off the desk, sat up and motioned for her to enter. "Thanks for sending a messenger to the driving range with the contract, Daze. How did you know I'd be there?"

She gave him a look that had "Oh, please" written all over it and sat down in one of his guest chairs.

"Right," he said, chuckling.

She crossed her legs, and her skirt rippled and flowed before it finally settled gently over her thighs. She leaned forward conspiratorially. "Okay," she said. "Tell me. How happy are you?"

"Unbelievably." Stop staring at her legs, he told himself. *Stop staring.*

"I know how you love to win," she said as she reached out and started compulsively straightening the knickknacks and pens and pads of paper on his desk. "But this one is important to you for other reasons, too, isn't it?"

"Yes, definitely," he said, then sidestepped her question by saying, "but I don't deserve all the credit. You put a lot of time in on this one, too."

She looked up from her organizing and her smile broadened. Daisy's smile radiated sheer sweetness, which was one of the many reasons his clients seemed to love her, as did every employee on the Mackenzie payroll. In fact, she'd been a boon to his growing business since the day she'd come into his office clutching the job posting from the university's career center.

When he'd first met Daisy, she'd been twenty-five years old and had been going to college part-time for several years. During the interview, they'd hit it off and he'd hired her on the spot. She'd been his first employee and had stuck with him the entire time he'd been building Mackenzie Architectural Revivals from a one-man show to a thirty-some-odd-employee, seven-figure-success story.

"It was a perfect case study for my senior business seminar," she reminded him as she sorted his pens into an antique silver loving cup he used as a holder.

As the pens rattled and clinked into place, he glanced at the jumble of sticky notes on his bulletin board. He sighed inwardly when he saw one that said, "Daisy's graduation, May 23." Two weeks ago. *Dammit.*

"Don't worry about it, Alec," she said as if reading his mind, which she did with spooky regularity. "In the end, I decided putting on a cap and gown and waltzing around with a bunch of twenty-somethings was silly. My dad and my brothers took me out to celebrate instead."

"Aren't you a twenty-something?"

She shrugged. "Chronologically."

"Well, anyway, I think this," he said as he leaned back in his big leather chair and pushed the contract to the center of his desk with a show of reverence that made her laugh, "calls for a celebration, too. Will you phone the Ivy and make reservations for tonight? Say, eight o'clock?"

Daisy dropped a pen onto the desk and flushed three shades of crimson. While it was a fact that Daisy Kincaid blushed more often than anyone he knew, he couldn't begin to imagine why making a dinner reservation would bring on a bout of it. Since he couldn't cook anything more complex than toasted bread, she'd made reservations for him more times than he cared to admit.

The blush stain was still on her cheeks when she got up abruptly and asked, "The Ivy in Santa Monica or Beverly Hills?"

"Beverly Hills, if you think it's possible on such short notice," he answered, and let her efficient manner chase away his concerns.

"No problem." Daisy stopped in the doorway as he picked up a pile of phone messages from his desk. "Oh, there's one in there from your mother. She called from Europe. No number but she said she'd try to call you later in the week."

"Mmm-hmm. Thanks." He found the message, crushed it with one hand and chucked it in the trashcan. Then he continued to flip through the rest of the slips of pink paper, barely noticing when the door snicked softly closed behind her.

Alec had just finished his Krispy Kremes and the interesting parts of the *Times* when Daisy returned. She walked into his office carrying a bright sticky note in one hand and a fresh cup of coffee in the other. As she came toward him, he got distracted by her legs again, this time by the length of them below that flippy, flowered skirt. It disoriented him so much that it took him a few beats to realize his gaze was fixed somewhere in the neighborhood of her sexy knees.

Sexy knees? he thought as he blinked hard, then looked away. What the hell was wrong with him? That was twice in one morning. And this was *Daisy,* for crying out loud. It had to be the long, hard hours they'd been working together to get the bid and the preliminary plans done for Santa Margarita. His social life had definitely atrophied over the past few months, and these bizarre thoughts about his assistant were unquestionably a sign that he needed to remedy that—and soon.

"Did you get some golf in this weekend?" he asked, grabbing the note and trying to get his thoughts back in order.

"Oh, I hacked around a bit with one of my brothers," she said with profound innocence as she set the steamy, fragrant coffee down on his desk and picked up the cup he'd already emptied.

"Uh-huh," he said. "Right." Daisy was no hacker. She was a scratch golfer—or so he'd learned when he'd asked her to fill in a foursome at Riviera a few weeks ago and she'd practically wiped the green with him.

As he stuck the note onto his bulletin board, he scanned it quickly. *"Ivy, 8:00 p.m., reservations for two, Mackenzie."*

"Alec, I was thinking I could—"

"Oh, wait," he said as he turned to pull his PalmPilot off the syncing cradle. "Could you call Heather Garrett for me and make sure she can make it at eight?" He turned back to hand the PDA to Daisy. "I just met her on Saturday night and—"

One look at Daisy's face and whatever he'd been saying went right out of his mind. Her bright smile had wilted, her forehead had creased into a deep frown, and this time she wasn't just flushed, she was bright red.

"Daisy?" he asked. "Are you okay?"

She hesitated, then took the PDA from his hand with the same enthusiasm one might normally display for a hissing cobra. "Of course." Her tone was flat, making the stormy glint in her dark eyes even more conspicuous. "Why?" she asked, and he was sure he heard a little quaver in her voice.

"You just look kind of…" He paused, studied her a minute. Daisy was never temperamental or cranky, so his concern was very real. "What were you going to say before?"

She stared at him, her expression blank.

"You said, 'I was thinking I could…'" he prompted.

After a long, searching look that inexplicably made him feel like he'd just been dissected and slipped under a microscope, she straightened up to her full five and a half feet and gave him a thin, unfamiliar smile. "I was thinking I needed to talk to you about something. But it can wait. I have some things I need to do first."

And before he could say another word, she turned and left his office.

What Daisy had to do didn't take very long. She went to her desk, slipped into her chair, pulled out the keyboard and carefully typed the memo that she should have written a year ago when she'd first realized she had a terrible, terminal crush on her boss.

While the laser printer hummed quietly, she stared at the familiar objects on her desk as if she'd never seen them before. There was a day planner, a Rolodex, dozens of photographs, a coffee cup with a handle shaped like a golf club, a candy dish full of fortunes she'd saved from lunches at the Chinese restaurant downstairs and a trophy Alec had given her when she'd co-captained the company's undefeated softball team with him.

She picked up the trophy and thought about all those evening practices, laughing with Alec and her co-workers, feeling a real sense of belonging and—if she were totally honest with herself—fantasizing that someday Alec would finally wake up, take her in his arms and declare his undying love for her. Right there on the diamond. In front of a crowd of corporate weekend warriors.

Ah, yes, she thought. Fantasies were lovely—at least until reality crashed in.

After lingering for another moment over both the trophy and her unrealized expectations, she set the prize back down on the desk with a noisy *thunk*. No sentimental baloney, she reminded herself as she put on her glasses, plucked the letter from the printer's tray and proofed it quickly. When she was satisfied, she slid the page into a waiting envelope and headed for Alec's office before she lost her nerve.

But as she reached for the doorknob, she paused for a second to gaze at her murky image reflected in the thick, opaque green glass that made up Alec's door. She acknowledged her familiar faults—not tall, not blond, not beautiful—but consoled herself that she had, as her salary had grown in the last few years, made something of an effort to buy more fashionable professional clothes and had even exchanged her haircuts at the local Quickie Cuts for a quarterly visit to an actual stylist.

She tugged at the hem of her short skirt and felt like an idiot for trying to dress to impress this morning. Maybe she was a late bloomer, or maybe growing up with just her father and three older brothers for role models had kept her from acquiring the requisite skills in cosmetics, fashion and flirting know-how. Whatever the cause, though, it still added up to the same thing: she was never going to snag the man she longed for.

Up until today she'd kept telling herself that it was just a matter of time. All she had to do was keep bringing him his Krispy Kremes, booking his travel plans, making his dinner reservations and picking up his dry cleaning. In her naïveté, she'd actually thought that if she kept doing all those things, he would eventually realize he couldn't live without her, both professionally *and* personally. But that was before this morning, before Alec had given her one final nudge out of the nest and she'd fallen from her fantasies to the cold, hard, unforgiving earth.

She sighed, smoothed her crisp, tailored suit jacket and gauzy skirt, straightened her glasses and told herself again that all that foolishness was over and done with. Then she turned the knob and marched confidently into Alec's beautiful, richly decorated office.

He didn't look up as she entered, and even though his dark head of wavy hair was tipped down, Daisy could imagine the concentration in his deep, indigo eyes. She noticed the way his black shirt hugged his strong shoulders as he scribbled notes on a quadrille pad. The well-developed arms she'd spent much too much time gawking at over the past couple of years flexed and tightened with the movement.

The sharp edge of the envelope dug into her palm as she clutched the letter. So what if he was a looker? She absolutely, positively, wasn't going to let that sway her now. She'd been hiding out behind this sweet, agreeable, I'll-wait-forever-for-you-to-notice-me facade far too long. It was time to be who she really was, so she put one hand on the sleek leather chair that faced his desk and cleared her throat firmly.

Alec looked up, stretched lazily and poured on that heart-melting smile of his, all white teeth and hot charm and oozing charisma. "Hey, Daze."

Normally that smile could make her stomach tighten and her heart go pitter-pat, but not anymore. Even a crush as stubborn as the one she had on Alec couldn't survive her humiliation when she'd realized he wasn't asking *her* to go to dinner to celebrate a job well done. It wasn't his fault, really, but she'd known at that very moment that she had to get the hell away from him. It was her only hope.

Without a word, she handed him the envelope, and his chair squeaked in protest as he reached out for it. "What's this?"

She squeezed the back of the chair so hard the smooth leather creaked beneath her grip. "My letter of resignation."

His smile shrank a little and one dark eyebrow shot up. "Now say, 'April fools.'"

In spite of her resolve to be strong, nervous waves kicked up in her stomach. "This isn't a joke, Alec."

Long, quiet seconds ticked by, one after another, but the silence was by no means calm. In fact, she started to imagine they were two gunfighters, each waiting for the other to twitch.

A moment later he caved when he unfolded his six-foot-plus frame and stood, looming over both his desk and her. "Aren't you happy here?"

A headache flowered behind her eyes and she wondered idly if there might be an oxygen shortage in the room. "That's irrelevant," she said, and the flatness of her own voice shocked her.

A muscle twitched at his jaw, his eyes darkened and narrowed. "Is it something I've done?"

Try something you haven't done, you dope, she wanted to shout, but said, simply, "No."

Alec used his fingers like a comb, dragging them through his incessantly messy, longish dark hair, but one disobedient wave of it fell back over one eye immediately. She stared at it, wishing—not for the first time—that it was her right and privilege to push it back into place.

"Well, I won't accept it." To punctuate his claim, he crumpled up the envelope and shot it into the trash can across the room.

A cold fist of frustration curled up inside her as she watched her carefully crafted resignation rebound off the credenza and sink gracefully for three points. Now that she was finished with the frantic pace of part-time school and a full-time job, she had more time than ever to contemplate the yawning stretch of futility that would be her life if she stayed here. Unless she made a change, she knew it would be more of the same—she would watch from the sidelines, powerless and lonely as he dated one bimbo after another and remained blissfully unaware of her as anything other than his loyal, hardworking assistant.

"I was actually just thinking that we'd have to change some things now that you're finished with school," he said, his voice low and relaxing and sure. "And this is as good a time as any to discuss it. Whatever it is you want, I'm sure we can work it out."

"You don't understand, Alec," she said, keeping her tone firm with substantial effort. "If you'd read that—" she jerked her head in the direction of the trash can "—you'd know that I'm giving two weeks notice. But I am leaving. I'm taking another job, one that is more in line with my career goals."

Since she hadn't actually taken another job, she experienced a tiny flash of guilt. Lies weren't her normal style, but she knew it was better this way. It would be a clean break and, more important, she wouldn't have to suffer the humiliation of telling him the real reason she was leaving.

As Alec stared at her, his eyes registered something that on anyone else she'd guess was hurt. Then he moved to the window and looked out over the short, featureless buildings to the ocean. He stood with his back to her, his hands on his hips, and his breathing was the only sound she could hear. He stayed there a moment, only a moment, but whatever it was that he saw beyond the glass triggered a change in his demeanor that shook her.

Because when he turned back to her, his blue eyes were icy, his mouth was drawn into a thin line. "It won't be necessary to give notice," he said, his voice as frosty as his gaze. "You can leave now."

She wouldn't have thought it was possible for her heart to sink further but it did, right down to the soles of her new summer sandals. Heat flooded her cheeks and the anxiety in her stomach revved up to a riot, but she managed to keep the flood of emotion out of her voice when she said, "I should at least finish out the day."

No particular expression lit his face as he said, "That won't be necessary."

Daisy bit her bottom lip to keep it from trembling. Dammit, this wasn't how it was supposed to end. Her heartbeat began to pound in her ears, but not so loudly that she couldn't hear the voice of some nameless, faceless coach from her sports-filled youth advise her with Obi-Wan-like wisdom, *Don't show weakness. Don't let 'em see how you really feel.*

A new resolve began to fill her, giving her strength. She stuck out her chin, put on a smile and threw out a hand for Alec to shake. "All right, then. I guess this is goodbye."

Alec's eyes were slightly glazed as he looked down at her outstretched hand. It was only after a long, long moment that he finally took it in his. His palm and fingers were rough and surprisingly work-worn, and the mere touch of them sent a ripple of warmth through her that shocked her so completely, she yanked her hand away as if it had been burned.

His eyes lit briefly with blue fire as he looked down at her, then they seemed to just…flicker out. Without another word, he turned away from her again.

She ran a hand down the front of her skirt absently and stole one last look at his familiar profile before forcing herself to walk out the door.

Now I know I've made the right decision, Daisy thought as she quickly threw as many things as she could into her tote and beelined for the elevator, rounding the cubicles that stood between her and escape as if she were running the final few yards of a marathon. He was bound to break her heart someday. Today was as good a day as any.

Once in the lobby, she hit the button to call the elevator before casting a quick glance at Nikki, receptionist and in-house gossip queen, who was holding the phone aloft and watching Daisy like she was going to be tested on the event later.

Daisy almost groaned out loud. During the last year, she'd often fantasized about ending her working relationship with Alec, but in her fantasies that ending had looked far more like an afternoon wedding by the sea than a cold, angry confrontation in his office.

When she entered the elevator, she pasted on a game smile for the receptionist.

"Are you coming back today?" Nikki asked, her dark eyes taking in Daisy's flushed skin and overflowing tote.

"No, definitely not," Daisy said, feeling a momentary flash of guilt at her evasion. While she and Nikki weren't particularly close, Daisy had made many friends at Mackenzie. She could only hope they wouldn't be worried about her when they found out she'd left without saying goodbye.

Thankfully, the elevator doors closed before Nikki could ask any more questions. And then Daisy Kincaid was left not only without a job, but without something she needed far more: the ever-present optimism that had made her think everything she wished for would come to her eventually if only she didn't give up.

Two

By the following afternoon, the coffee was charred, the copy machine was broken, the blueprints were late, and no one in the entire office had a clue about how to contact the maintenance guy to come turn off the emergency exit alarm that was clanging both inside and outside Alec's head.

He was just taking a deep breath and trying to decide which crisis to deal with first when the alarm suddenly quieted. *Good.* At least one thing had been handled, even without the help of the woman he was only just now realizing had been the friggin' beating heart of his company.

He stifled a curse, the same one he'd been muttering ever since Daisy had handed him her resignation and run out of the office with all that stuff she kept on her desk spilling out of her bag. He remembered now how he'd stood in his doorway and watched her go while the scent of her had still hung in the air around him. Cookies and warm milk. How could anyone smell like cookies and warm milk? he'd thought then, even as something unfamiliar inside him had urged him to run after her.

He hadn't, of course. After all, it wasn't the first time he'd watched the door close behind someone he cared about.

Still, he couldn't quite believe she was gone. Over the years he and Daisy had worked countless late nights together, had hundreds of early-morning conference calls, organized dozens of groundbreaking celebrations, even shared birthday lunches at her favorite Chinese restaurant downstairs. The very idea that she could quit like that—without any discussion or explanation, without even giving him a chance to tell her how important she was to him and the company. After all they'd been through together...well, it still stung, that was all.

Move on, Mackenzie, he told himself as he pulled the next potential emergency off the top of his phone message pile. He should be used to the important people in his life bailing out on him by now. He would just put Daisy out of his mind and focus instead on deciphering the loopy handwriting of the gum-chomping teenager the temp agency had sent him this morning.

The phone on his desk rang five shrill rings before he saw the light begin to shine steadily.

"You have a call," the temp murmured languidly via the intercom.

"No kidding," he mumbled as he reached for his phone. "Mackenzie," he growled into the receiver.

"Alec? My God, boy. Who was that woman? She was so rude."

Could this day get any worse? "Good afternoon, Mr. Baldwin," Alec said, cooling his temper as he prepared to soothe his most important client.

The normally placid Joseph Baldwin, the man responsible for awarding Alec's firm the contract for the Santa Margarita project, sounded flustered when he said, "Where's Daisy? She's not sick, is she?"

Intellectually, Alec knew grinding his teeth wouldn't help, but it seemed this week was destined to head downhill in a cart with no brakes. "No, no. Daisy's left the company," he said casually, but the sound of it in his own ears gave him a sharp pain.

Worse, his bleak announcement was met with an unnerving silence from Baldwin. Alec glanced at the latest issue of the industry's most important magazine, *Architectural Abstracts,* and was reminded that Baldwin was the golden key Alec needed to prove himself once and for all to his critics.

"Left for good, son?"

"It seems so." Alec rubbed one aching temple. For the dozenth time that day, he told himself he should belly up to the bar, go find her and drag her back here. But he discarded the idea just as he had ten minutes ago and ten minutes before that. He'd never crawled to anyone in his life and he wasn't going to start now—even if the "crawlee" was the best assistant he'd ever had.

He had no idea how he was going to replace her. Over the years, she'd become his right-hand man—or, more appropriately, his right-hand *woman.* In addition to keeping his personal life running smoothly, she'd taken on more and more business responsibilities, doing everything from purchasing to negotiating to preparing bids.

Anyway, none of that mattered now, Alec thought as he

tuned back in just as Baldwin was saying, "I have to be honest with you, son. If you could allow a diamond like her to slip away, my confidence in your judgment is shaken. My wife has a sort of sixth sense about people, and she sees a lot of potential in the girl. In fact, Virginia has decided to stay on the island during reconstruction just to work with Daisy on the project."

This time Alec did grind his teeth. "I can see I wasn't clear about the depth of Mrs. Baldwin's feelings for Daisy," Alec said carefully. "But you should know that while Daisy would have been an important part of the project, she wasn't scheduled to be on the island, anyway."

"We put it in the contract that she would be."

Alec looked down at the thick contract that he hadn't had time to finish reviewing even though he should have had it signed and back in Baldwin's hands this morning.

"I thought you knew that her input and organizational talent were factors in selecting Mackenzie," Mr. Baldwin continued. "Virginia sees the renovation of the mansions on Santa Margarita as the chance to cement her family's legacy. I don't think…"

It had been clear to Alec since his first meeting with the Baldwins that it was Virginia Baldwin who called the shots, so it didn't take a genius to guess the man didn't want to face his wife with the news of Daisy's departure. Alec almost felt sorry for him.

"I understand what you're saying." *But there's no way I'm going to run after her. No way.*

There was another long, disturbing silence that let him know Mr. Baldwin's ah-shucks routine had grown very thin. "All right, son. Tell you what. Call me by the end of the day so I'll know whether to go back to the other bids for our project."

And just like that, Alec's blood turned icy cold. *Other bids?* Without a signed contract, Baldwin was certainly within his rights to go back to bid. Alec could think of several of his competitors who would kill or die to wrench the Santa Margarita deal out of his stunned grip. His own best friend would be dancing on Alec's professional grave by Happy Hour if he heard there was a chance the project was up for grabs.

Alec glanced again at the issue of *Architectural Abstracts,* the one that had come out just yesterday with an unpleasant article about his work entitled "The Dilettante Designer," which had implied that his success was more a result of his family's money and connections than his own talent.

He tugged an agitated hand through his hair. Well, he was going to stuff the evidence of his talent down that writer's sleazy, lying throat soon enough, and to do that he needed the Santa Margarita project more than ever. He'd be damned if he'd let any other architect on earth have a shot at this job. After all, nothing less than his career and the respect of his professional community were hanging in the balance.

The phone's receiver bit into his hand as he gripped it. The only word he could manage as his mind began to wrap around what he now had to do was "Understood."

He could almost feel Baldwin releasing a long-held breath. "Fine. Wonderful," he said, and his voice was light as he said his goodbyes.

Alec hung up and headed for the elevator before he had time to rethink what he was about to do. In the grand scheme of things, this was merely a speed bump, he told himself as he hit the down button. He'd get Daisy back, then she could pack up their office and relocate to Santa Margarita with him for the duration of the job. That would keep her from flying the coop while he wasn't looking *and* give Mrs. Baldwin what she wanted.

"Will you be back today, Mr. Mackenzie?" Nikki called from behind the reception desk.

"Probably." He glanced at the girl over his shoulder, then muttered to himself, "Unless the little fugitive gives me trouble."

"Excuse me?" Nikki asked as she practically fell over the desk in her efforts to hear him.

"Just talking to myself."

As he rode the elevator down to the garage, the sadness he'd seen behind the determination in Daisy's eyes the day before flashed into his mind. More disturbing, that image was followed closely by the memory of her velvety skin on his just before she'd pulled her hand away.

Alec cursed under his breath and swept the unsettling thoughts from his mind. Then he got into his car, gunned the engine and peeled out of the parking garage. Nothing mattered now except securing the Santa Margarita contract. And to do that, he had to do something he said he'd never do, something he wasn't even sure he knew how to do.

Grovel.

"Money?" Daisy Kincaid repeated the word into the phone she had tucked between her ear and her shoulder.

"Yes," her oldest brother, Tom, answered with longsuffering patience. "Green stuff? Exchangeable for goods and services worldwide? You've heard of it, surely."

"Very funny. You know what a miser I am. My savings will float me," she said as she looked around her drop-cloth-draped kitchen which was strewn with paint cans and pans and brushes. "That is, if I stop my midnight runs to the twenty-four-hour Home Depot."

"Oh, good Lord. Tell me you're not painting again."

"Uh," she stalled. "Did I say I was painting?"

"Daze, your house is going to start looking like a kaleidoscope if you open a can of paint every time you get stressed out."

"I'm not stressed out," she said, and her stomach chose that moment to remind her she hadn't eaten since yesterday. She sighed, then wrapped her brush in plastic wrap so it wouldn't dry out and climbed down the ladder. "I'm just reviewing my options."

Tom was quiet a moment, and she could almost see his mouth twisting into a who-are-you-trying-to-kid frown. "I thought you said you already had an offer."

"I do," she said, then added sheepishly, "sort of." Over the years, she'd had many offers from both colleagues and competitors of Alec's, so all she really had to do was get out some résumés. She knew for sure that Todd Herly would love to get his hands on her, if only to win one more round in the friendliest feud in history. Somehow, though, the prospect of working anywhere but Mackenzie depressed her.

She opened a can of tuna, gave the fishy smelling water to her cat, Bam Bam, then quickly put together a sandwich as Tom, the most responsible of her three older brothers, began a long-winded, well-intentioned lecture.

Out of habit, she listened to him yammer on as she ate, even though her mind was in the next county. What she was really thinking about was that on a normal Tuesday afternoon she'd be grabbing bites of a brown sack lunch at her desk instead of stenciling the trim around her kitchen cabinets and listening to her brother. But nothing about her life was normal, she thought as Bam Bam looked up at her, blinked lazily and licked his chops. No job, no income, no Alec.

"I've got a handle on it, Tom," she said, feeling suddenly tired. "I've got résumés ready to go to my two best prospects and I have a Rolodex full of business cards from Alec's colleagues. Some of them have been trying to poach me since the beginning."

Tom laughed. "Good. That ought to send Mackenzie off his hinges. At least it'll give him something to think about before he starts taking his next assistant for granted."

Daisy tried not to think about how Alec probably wouldn't care at all. Surely he'd seen his business associates slipping her their business cards at meetings and ground breakings and grand opening parties and saying things like, "If you ever decide to leave this bum, blah, blah, blah." At the time, she'd just laughed and filed the information away for a rainy day, but now…

Well, now it was pouring. In buckets.

"If it makes you happy, I'll place a few more calls when I'm done here," she said as she cleaned and put away the dishes in that compulsive way she wished she could stop but never could.

"Good. And call if you need anything. *Anything,* you hear? You've been doing for other people long enough. Let someone help you for a change."

She promised that she would before she hung up, then she climbed the ladder and unwrapped her brush.

What was she waiting for? she asked herself as she dipped the short bristles into a jar of thick paint. She should be happy to be moving on in her career. After all, being someone's assistant wasn't why she'd worked so hard to put herself through college. And it wasn't why she'd stuck it out even in the face of holding down a full-time job and taking care of her father and older brothers.

No, she'd done all that because she had a dream, a dream that she refused to abandon just because she was currently stuck on one of life's sandbars. Once she'd saved enough money, she was going to take her business know-how and her passion for taking care of people and she was going to pour it all into owning and running her own bed-and-breakfast. She knew she had a long way to go and many things to learn yet but she was still hanging on tightly to the vision she had for her inn. After all, she'd been tinkering with it ever since she was eight years old and her mother had taken her to stay at one of Santa Barbara's best B&Bs—a trip that unexpectedly had turned out to be their last "girls only" weekend together before her mom had passed away.

Daisy sighed, brushed a strand of hair out of her eyes with her wrist and refocused on the situation at hand. Now that she'd left Mackenzie, she realized that she'd been staying on there for two reasons she was not proud of: an unrequited crush and a salary she'd be hard-pressed to make anywhere else. The first one she'd put behind her the moment she'd seen Alec's eyes turn hard and brittle as he essentially told her to take her two-weeks' notice and stick it. The second one she knew she would eventually, through diligence and determination, replace.

So what *was* she waiting for? And even as she asked herself, she realized she'd known the answer since she'd walked out of Alec's office. In her deepest-held fantasies, she was still waiting for him to run over here, drop to one knee, tell her he couldn't live without her and beg her to come back.

But since it was pretty clear that wasn't going to happen, she knew it was time to buckle down and find another job *tout de suite.*

As soon as she finished this coat of paint.

"You certainly have been busy," a deep voice said from behind her.

Daisy jumped, jerked sideways to look over her shoulder and saw Alec, then panicked when her quick movement caused the ladder to teeter unsteadily. "Alec!" she yelped as she clutched desperately at the rough wood, heard the clatter of the brush when it hit the countertop below her. In a split second of pure terror, the ladder pitched one way, she pitched the other, and the battle was lost. She prayed, she cursed— and then fell right into Alec's waiting arms.

So much for fantasies.

"Oof!" Her lungs emptied in one painful rush and she gasped, sucking oxygen in through clenched teeth. She heard Alec swallow a muffled curse and felt him stagger back a step, forcing her to wrap her arms around his neck and hold on to try to keep from falling again. Her face burned hotly as the strong arms that held her tightened and drew her closer and, just like that, her need for fresh air was forgotten.

Daisy's senses tingled and popped as Alec held her close with one arm, supported her bare, paint-spattered legs with the other and steadied them both. She felt the steely muscles of his shoulder flexing beneath her cheek, smelled his very masculine scent that she knew instinctively had nothing to do with cologne, saw the thudding of his heart pulsing beneath the stubble at his jaw.

They only stood like that for a moment, but as they did, neither of them relaxed their hold. For that time, standing there in a kitchen that smelled of fresh paint and tuna sandwiches, the world hung suspended like ripe fruit weighing down a slender branch.

"Degree of difficulty," Alec said finally, affecting a sports announcer's voice, "8.5."

She laughed. She couldn't help it. "I think the Russian judges are going to give you extra points for that catch, Alec."

"I'll take all the extra points I can get," he said in a heavy, sexy voice that sent spirals of heat zooming through her, licking at her in places she wished it wouldn't.

Daisy squirmed. "You can…" She swallowed thickly, both dreading the moment's end and anxious to see what would happen if it didn't. "You can let me down now."

His face was close, his expression guarded, but the corners of his mouth had crept up subtly and his blue eyes had taken on a wicked gleam. For a second, she had a strange feeling he was going to refuse but then he gently released her legs and held her close while he eased her slowly down the front of his strong, muscled length.

Her damned double-crossing body caught fire as his hands moved down her back, slipping lower and lower as he guided her to the ground, until finally he was almost touching her butt. Breathing had practically become an Olympic sport in and of itself by the time her feet finally, mercifully, touched the cold tile floor and she stumbled back against the counter.

She reached behind her and gripped the edge of the countertop, watching as he shoved his hands into the pockets of his stylishly worn-out jeans.

"Not at the new job yet, huh?" he asked, and his composed manner was so at odds with her own flustered one that it drove her kind of crazy.

"You gave me a two-week vacation I wasn't expecting, remember?" she reminded him with a synthetic smile.

"Ah, yes. There is that." He looked around the kitchen. "I can sure think of better ways to spend a vacation than this, though."

"I'm sure you can," she said, sweetness coating each word. "But planning time was woefully short."

Alec's answering smile was a cool, gorgeous stretch across his face. She stared at his mouth and felt a flush of pleasure sweep through her as she imagined his lips on hers, his hands caressing her, his chest pressed up against hers. And suddenly she realized she hadn't put her crush quite as far behind her as she'd previously thought.

That awareness shocked her into action. Forcing back a wave of unwanted desire, Daisy struggled to organize her thoughts. What was he doing here? Had he come to apologize as she'd hoped? And, most important of all, what the hell had just happened between them?

Their last conversation—and the humiliating event that had sparked it—careened back into her mind, dispelling the rosy glow she was already using to color the encounter they'd just shared. "Why are you here, Alec? What do you want?"

Alec watched Daisy lean back against the counter and saw the full, firm breasts he'd never known were hiding beneath her conservative work clothes straining against her T-shirt. At that moment he knew exactly what he wanted, and that realization made him want to turn around and run out of her house before he slipped up and did something about it.

But he couldn't run away, not this time, so he drank his fill, surveying her from her bare feet and her long tanned legs to her denim cutoffs and a T-shirt that molded those tempting breasts and revealed a sliver of her flat stomach.

It was, by far, the sexiest handyman get-up he'd ever seen.

But in the next moment he savagely exorcised those thoughts. So what if he suddenly found her attractive? The timing stunk, no question about it, and the last thing he needed was to complicate their situation further. After all, it was common knowledge on Nikki's grapevine that Daisy was planning a love-marriage-children combo at some point in her future. And that was a concept that ran just slightly counter to Alec's own commitment-free, casual-sex, eternal-independence plan. Alec went out with women who understood that, and if for some reason they forgot, their relationship usually wound down in a hurry.

Anyway, he was here to grovel, he reminded himself, letting the thought resurrect the hurt and anger he'd felt when she'd deserted him—and the frustration he'd felt at having to give in to Joseph Baldwin's demands.

"Daisy," he said simply, his voice harder and louder and harsher than he'd meant it to be. "I want you to come back to work."

Her expression shifted and altered, as if she were trying to understand a language she'd only just learned. She tipped her head to the side and considered him. "This is quite a change of heart for you, isn't it? Just yesterday, you pretty much told me not to let the door smack me on the butt on the way out."

The memory of how the swell of her butt had just felt under his hands rushed back, making him smile when he didn't feel like smiling at all. "I have a hot temper. You know that—"

"You do not," she scoffed. "You're the most even-tempered man I know." She narrowed her eyes and peered closer at him. "Unless it's a Jekyll and Hyde thing you've been bottling up all this time."

Clearly she was going to make swallowing a whole crow very hard. "Actually," he said, beginning to enjoy their sparring in spite of himself. "I think I can honestly say I'm not a schizophrenic madman."

She made a show of being relieved. "Well, that's reassuring."

"Daisy, come back to work," he said, stepping toward her. "I need you."

She pressed herself against the counter and it made him feel like a bully. "I told you I can't do that," she said.

The quick refusal surprised him, although he knew it shouldn't. In the past twenty-four hours, he'd learned more about Daisy Kincaid's stubborn streak than he had in the previous three years. "Why can't you?"

The same sadness he'd glimpsed the other day flickered in her eyes, then she shook her head. "Why can't you just let it alone?"

He watched as a few dark curls escaped her loose ponytail and tumbled down to frame her face. "Listen, I'll give you whatever you want," he said, his gaze fixated on a cinnamon-colored curl. "An office. A raise. Whatever you need."

A thoughtful light replaced the sadness in her eyes for a moment and he hurried to press his advantage. "I'll double your salary. Hell, I'll double whatever offer you've got from…who did you say you took a job with?"

Her mouth tightened into a frown. "I didn't. And this isn't about money, Alec," she said, and something about the tone of her voice let him know that avenue was closed. "Besides, I'm done with being an assistant."

"You want a different job? No problem. What do you want it to be?" Even as he said it, the salesmanship in his own voice made him cringe.

She must have heard it, too, because she gave him a suspicious look. "What's going on, Alec?"

"Listen," he said, backing off a bit. "Just come to Santa Margarita with me. We can figure it out from there."

At that, excitement touched every feature on her pretty face. "Santa Margarita? What do you mean?"

Relief filled him. *He had her. This is going to work.* "Didn't I tell you? I want you to come with me."

She bit into her soft bottom lip and considered his invitation. Her mouth was full but not lush, her teeth straight and white. As he stared, he felt his breath go shallow and his body respond to the temptation of her nearness.

Daisy opened her mouth to speak, then closed it, shaking her head. Her hesitation was downright endearing. It made him feel like a heel.

"I can't be your assistant anymore, Alec," she said finally.

"You don't have to be my assistant," he said as if that concept were preposterous. What could he offer her that was attractive enough to entice her back? *Think, Mackenzie.* Just because groveling wasn't on his résumé didn't mean he couldn't figure this out. "You have your business degree now, right?" he asked and she nodded. "You can run the business office. Problem solved."

She looked down at the fallen ladder and the paint splotch

where the brush had hit the tile counter. She bent to right the ladder, and the soft denim of her shorts did something sinful to her rear. His pulse spiked as he watched her, and frankly it made him incredibly uneasy.

"You couldn't do it," she said as she ripped a paper towel from its holder and wiped the countertop with hard, jerky strokes. "I'd be back to making your dinner reservations and picking up your dry cleaning in no time."

Something in her words nagged at his conscience, but the feeling fled as desperation fogged up his mind. "Daze, if it's a deal breaker, I'll make *your* dinner reservations and pick up *your* dry cleaning."

The hand that held the paper towel stilled as she regarded him with a sly smile. But then she looked down at her bare feet and her unpolished toenails and shook her head again.

"I'm sorry," she said. "My answer is still no."

A giant steel band tightened around his chest when he came to stand before her and took her hands in his. Her scent enveloped him, so sweet and familiar that for one insane moment he almost pulled her closer. But instead, he drew in a deep, satisfying breath and waited until she'd lifted her eyes to meet his. "Daisy, I don't know how else to say this." His throat felt strangely tight, so tight he had to clear it before he continued. "I need you. I can't do this without you. Please."

And it wasn't until he'd said the words that he realized he really meant them. He did need her. She was as integral to his business as his CAD program, his laptop, his cell phone and his PDA. What had he been thinking of to let her go?

She wasn't wearing her glasses. This close, her eyes looked huge, soulful. She held his gaze unflinchingly, and the intensity made him feel like he was somehow being pulled inside her. Damn, where had this woman been hiding all these years?

Finally she withdrew her hands from his, tucked them into the back pockets of her frayed cutoffs and nearly leveled him with a single look. "Okay, Alec," she said on a sigh. "You're not going to like it, but these are my nonnegotiable terms."

He steeled himself for what was to come even as he rejoiced that the Santa Margarita project was his again. It didn't matter anymore that the Baldwins had leaned on him to get her back. Now that he knew she was coming with him, he realized he was actually glad they'd forced his hand.

"I'll take the raise and I'll take a new position with Mackenzie." She sucked in a quick breath. "But I want to be your partner, the co-manager of the entire job."

He stared at her, the relief seeping out of him bit by bit. "Partner? Co-manager? But you—"

She held up a hand to silence him. "Listen, my duties are going to look very much like what I've been doing for you for the past few years, only I've been doing it without the title." Her look dared him to deny it, and since he couldn't, he remained silent. "So here's the plan," she said. "I'll run the business side and you'll run the design side. But you'll have to involve me in every aspect of the job and you'll have to respect my decisions. And," she said with what he thought might be a little tremble in her voice, "when we're done in Santa Margarita, I'm leaving Mackenzie for good."

A hard, unforgiving mass settled in his stomach. He knew he should be happy, but how could he? For one thing, Santa Margarita was the most important, most complicated job he'd taken on in the three years he'd been in business for himself.

He couldn't accept her terms. It just didn't make sense. It was nuts to even consider it.

Powerlessness gnawed at him. With a few rare exceptions, his life had been like one long limo ride—taking him where he wanted to go, whenever he wanted to go there. He'd been indulged in all the ways that mattered by his absentee parents, and later he'd made sure he denied himself nothing, as well.

For him, life was clear-cut: he got what he wanted. Which made this compromise feel like a very dangerous journey into a great, uncharted wilderness.

But it appeared he had no choice. He'd simply have to manage her as closely as she managed the job. Not that managing her closely would be a hardship exactly, he thought as he stared at the light glinting off her soft hair, at the deep vee of her T-shirt and everything it revealed—

"Is it a deal, Alec?" she asked, interrupting his wayward thoughts as she thrust out a hand.

He took it automatically and held it in his own for a moment. It was warm, her skin was terribly soft and he knew he was in trouble. "Tell me again what I'm agreeing to?"

"A raise, the comanager position, respect for my decisions, the freedom to leave at the end of the project and that other thing you offered."

He frowned. "What other thing?"

A perfect smile stole across her face. "C'mon. You couldn't have forgotten already."

Desperation had lured him into giving away the farm, that was for sure, but when he searched his memory for anything else he'd offered, he came up empty. He shook his head. "Remind me."

She pumped his hand in a firm handshake. "You offered to be my errand boy," she said with that relentlessly cheery smile. "And, believe me, Alec, that *is* a deal breaker."

Three

Daisy was still smiling three days later as she gazed out beyond the helicopter's enormous curved front windows and took in the vastness of the shimmering Pacific Ocean below. She simply couldn't believe the turns her life had taken in the past week. From love-besotted fool and unemployed home-improvement junkie to ruthless negotiator and comanager of a coveted architectural redesign project all in a matter of days.

Now that's what she called progress.

She cast a quick glance over her shoulder. Alec sat in the helicopter's back seat, tapping away at his laptop. Their luggage was piled high on the seat beside him and Bam Bam was in a cat carrier at his feet.

Alec didn't look up, but she was starting to get used to that. In the last few days since he'd left her kitchen with her list of conditions stuck in his craw, their relationship had been strictly business. From the moment she'd walked back into the office the next day until they'd stepped into this helicopter ten minutes ago, she'd been working with a stranger.

In fact, the changes in their relationship were so striking that she found she couldn't even enjoy some of his initial errand boy gaffes. The process of securing this helicopter charter, for instance, should have been hilarious. After all, shortly after their arrival at the Long Beach airport, it had become very clear that Alec thought that helicopters were standing by to take commuters to Santa Margarita in the same abundance as taxis waited at the airport's curb. But after forty tense minutes—when he'd finally found and bribed an off-duty pilot he'd chased down on the tarmac—she realized she had a weak stomach for revenge. Not, she thought with a quick grin, that she was going to let him off the hook. He'd made a promise and she was going to enjoy it.

She sighed. In a way, their new relationship was all for the best. When she'd committed to the project, she'd firmly placed her pathetic crush in the bottom drawer of her emotional file cabinet. Now all she really wanted from Alec was the opportunity to do an extraordinary job so she could enrich both her résumé and her bank account—and get the invaluable experience that would help her get one step closer to her dream.

And I'll just keep telling myself that every time I encounter that bone-melting smile of his.

The pilot, a thirty-ish, sun drenched, California-cool character named Troy reached over and touched her knee, then pointed out the front window. "There's the island," she heard him say through the elaborate headset that allowed all three of them to communicate freely despite the scream of the turbine engine.

Her breath hitched as the coastline of the small, lush island came into view. From their vantage point, the hills and valleys looked seductive and curvaceous, one flowing into the next like soft waves. Instinct drove her to look back at Alec to see his reaction but wasn't really surprised to see his head was still tipped down over his laptop.

"Alec," she said into the microphone that hovered near her lips. "Look. Isn't it beautiful?"

When he looked up at her, his jaw was set so tight she wished she could see what was in his eyes behind those dark sunglasses. "I can't see quite as much from back here," he said flatly, then returned to his task.

Oh-kay, she thought. So the distance between them was going to take a lot of getting used to. But no matter what, she absolutely was not going to slip back into the role of his adoring doormat. She simply couldn't.

"Well, you can have shotgun next time," she said cheerfully, then turned back around, intent on enjoying her first helicopter flight in spite of Alec's sour mood.

"You see all those buildings around the bay down there?" Troy asked. "That's the town of Paloma. It's not much to look at from here, but it's Santa Margarita's biggest town and its main port."

"Do you live there?" Her voice sounded muffled in her headset, but the knowledge that Alec could hear every word she was saying made her nervous and heightened her pitch.

Troy nodded. "My friends and I have rented a place in town for years, but I only live here full-time in the spring and summer. The resident business is slow and it's worse in the off season."

"We were lucky you were headed home this afternoon. I don't think there were any more charters available today."

"You got that right," he said, and rewarded her with a big grin. The contrast of his white teeth against his tanned skin was stunning. He looked like something out of a J. Crew catalog. "And I got to make a little extra cash. Looks like I'll be able to stock the bar for our party tonight after all. Hey," he said, "if you guys want to come…"

Alec made a choking sound, but she ignored him and said, "That's sweet of you, Troy."

"But we're here to work," Alec added in a growly voice.

"Oh, you've got to take some time off," Troy went on, undeterred. "I've got a friend who runs the Jet-Ski concession at the dock." He looked over at Daisy. "Maybe we could go out one day. What do you say?"

While Daisy was no expert on the matter, she was pretty sure Troy was flirting with her and, dammit, she was going to enjoy it. Just because Alec had never noticed her didn't mean she had to die on the vine, did it?

She turned her back on Alec, put on her friendliest smile and said, "I'd love to." Then, resisting the temptation to see how her mutiny had landed in the back seat, she continued to chat with their pilot about island life.

Well, at least she'd have one friend here, she thought as they talked on as if Alec had fallen out of the helicopter a few miles back. No, two friends, she amended. She'd had several great phone conversations with Mrs. Baldwin in the last few days. The older woman, who'd insisted on being called Virginia, hadn't seemed surprised that Daisy was coming along, nor had she seemed particularly surprised when she'd been told about Daisy's new position.

"Good for you," Virginia had said. "People grow in extraordinary ways when they're handed a big challenge."

Daisy loved that Virginia Baldwin was going to be her friend. She had a soft spot for kindly, mothering types, and it didn't take an analyst's couch to figure out why.

"Almost there," Troy said, then pointed to the island. "Hey, check it out. Buffalo."

Daisy looked down to see a herd of the lumbering, dark, shaggy beasts roaming a hilltop and felt as if she were flying over a Remington painting. "Are they friendly?"

"I don't know any personally," Troy said with a wink. "But I've heard they're in a bad mood most of the time."

As he spoke, the airport came into view, a tiny paved oasis on a mountaintop which lay roughly at the center of the dog-legged island. Several small buildings were scattered beside the runway and there was one larger building that had Buffalo Bill's painted in huge letters on its roof.

"Best buffalo burgers on earth right there," Troy said as he hovered the noisy copter above the helipad that jutted out from the runway at an angle. "And forty different kinds of beer." His words were almost drowned out by the thwackity-thwacking of the blades as they landed. "Hang on just a minute until I get her shut down, then I'll get you both out of here."

As the turbines whirred down, Daisy chanced one more look at Alec. He was still poring over his computer, seemingly oblivious to the world around him—except for that muscle jumping at his jaw. That, she knew from years of working at his side, was a sign that he was very much aware of his surroundings—and that he was very much annoyed by them.

Alec was positive that he was going to grind his teeth down to powder if he didn't get out of this noisy, glass purgatory really soon. For starters, the junior-high style flirting going on up front for the past twenty minutes had been driving him freaking crazy. Who did that aging surf rat think he was? For all Troy knew, he and Daisy were a couple, for chrissakes. They weren't, of course, but what made him think Daisy was the, "Hey, wanna come to a kegger?" type, anyway?

And as for her, what was with all the blushing and giggling and "Oh, Troy"ing? Didn't she know what guys like that wanted from a girl like her? And he shouldn't even get started on what she was wearing. The heat rose in his veins as he took another look at her form-fitting black pants and high boots that made her legs look miles long and that sleeveless shirt that both clung to her toned back and made her breasts look—

"Sir?" Troy said, pulling him from his dangerous thoughts. Alec looked to his left and saw that Daisy's new little friend had opened the door and was extending a hand to help him out of the helicopter.

Oh, hell no, Alec thought as he picked up the cat cage and thrust it at Troy. The cat hissed at Alec and took a swipe at the bars of the little prison. "Here. And the luggage, if it's not too much trouble," he said, ignoring the cat and tipping his head toward the leaning tower of black leather and canvas to his right.

"Sure, sir," Troy said, setting the cage down next to the now quiet helicopter. "Let me just help Daisy first."

And before Alec could say another word, Troy had

sprinted around the front of the helicopter and opened Daisy's door. Alec watched as the their pilot reached up and put his hands on Daisy's waist, watched as she grinned down at him, watched as she laughed and let herself be lowered to the ground.

Three months. He and Daisy were going to be on this island together for three long months. Suddenly, without even understanding why, he felt like he'd been consigned to an eternity in hell.

Twenty-five endless minutes later, after winding down a narrow road lined plentifully with wild sumac and other assorted weeds, their shuttle bus came to a halt in front of the Hotel Margarita which was nestled up against the foothills of Paloma. Fortunately, Alec had been spared the company of Troy who'd elected to stay for "a coupla brewskis" up at the airport. *Un*fortunately, they hadn't gotten away before their pilot had given Daisy directions to the party he and his friends were hosting later that night.

"Oh, Alec," Daisy said as she emerged from the bus behind him. "It's beautiful."

Alec, who had somehow managed to sign himself up to be Daisy's damn Sherpa during their negotiation, stopped stacking their luggage long enough to look up at the quaint Spanish Revival structure, its balconies strewn with bright bougainvillea, its courtyard lush and vibrant. Even through his annoyance, his artist's eye couldn't fail to see the charm of the place.

He glanced at Daisy and saw her face sparkling with excitement and knew he was being a world-class jerk. But he also knew that this distance between them was necessary.

After he'd left Daisy's house the other day, he'd spent the rest of the afternoon at the driving range trying to force her from his mind. It didn't work even a little bit, and as he'd sped along Pacific Coast Highway toward home, he'd finally had to admit to himself that his attraction to her wasn't going to go away. Which was *insane* since she'd quit on him and held him hostage with that long list of provisos and was making his life miserable by taking advantage of his stupid offer to do her errands. And besides, she was the wrong kind of woman. Wrong, wrong, wrong.

So that was why, sometime between standing in her kitchen negotiating their deal and arriving at the office the following morning, he'd decided that keeping their relationship rigidly businesslike was the best and safest route. And he was confident that he could maintain an all-business, all-the-time, no-nonsense relationship with her, no matter how great her rear end looked in those pants or how her dark hair—normally pinned back tight—was now tumbling down her back in curly waves or how her legs—

"Why don't you go inside and check us in," he said, turning away. "It's under my name."

When Daisy returned a few minutes later, he noticed she was worrying that bottom lip of hers with her teeth as she approached. He'd known her long enough to know that was a bad sign. "What?" he asked.

"I got our key," she said, dangling a key chain shaped like a margarita glass from her fingertips. *"Key,"* she emphasized and her meaning began to sink in.

In spite of the mild, summer temperature, Alec went cold. "Tell me the other rooms aren't ready yet, please."

She shook her head and her silly curls bobbed and danced

about. "Apparently, you booked their suite," she said as she bent down and stuck her fingers between the bars of her cat's cage and made a kissing noise that was so distracting he almost forgot what they were talking about. "Although Bill— he's the desk manager—says we're really going to like the layout. Two sleeping areas off one common room which we can use as our office and—" she glanced up at him "—one bathroom."

"Didn't you ask if they had anything else?" The panic in his voice was plain even to him.

She shot him that "Oh, please" look she did so well. "Of course, but they don't have anything right now. Bill says they may be able to find us another room in about a week but this is the beginning of the high season on an island that desperately needs hotel space. Unless we have another solution for our field office, this is it." The key dangled from her fingers, taunting him for his ham-fisted handling of their arrangements so far. "If you'd like some training for your new assistant position, Alec," she said with a smug smile, "you should let me know."

He let his gaze wander from the key in her hand, up her lean, tanned arm, to her shoulder and long, slender neck, then up to her mouth where, he noticed, she'd applied a hint of pale lipstick. Her lips were full, shaped like a cupid's bow and were so thoroughly kissable he couldn't believe he'd never seen it before. How could she have changed so fast? And, dammit, why'd she have to do it now?

"So…" Her voice was tight and breathy, making him look up to see what was wrong. Her widened eyes, her flushed cheeks and her crinkled brow were all it took to let him know he'd been staring.

He felt like a high school boy caught looking up the cheer-leader's skirt. He cleared his throat and grabbed as many bags as he could gather with both hands. "Looks like we're going to be stuck with it for a while," he said and indicated that she should precede him with a tip of his chin. "Let's go see how bad it really is."

Daisy's amusement at Alec's inability to plan anything more complicated than getting out of bed in the morning died a few minutes later when she saw where they were going to be staying for the time being.

Actually, she thought as she walked across the cool, tiled floor, if not for the fact that she had no intention of spending the summer sleeping anywhere near him, the suite would have been perfect. The common room would be a great field office—large and full of light, it had three big tables, a few upholstered chairs, and enough space for all the equipment Alec had hopefully arranged to have shipped over. A quaint kitchenette was tucked almost out of sight at the back of the suite and a little garden lay beyond two immense French doors that faced the sea.

The rest of it, though, was a problem. The bedrooms, while nicely appointed, were essentially separated by only a dressing area and a large, well-equipped bathroom.

Alec rapped at a shared wall, testing for solidity and, pre-sumably, soundproofing. "You don't snore, do you?"

"I wouldn't know," she said absently as she peered into a closet.

"None of your boyfriends have ever mentioned it?"

"I've never…" Wait a dang minute, she thought as she closed the closet door with a thud. She didn't have to tell him any of the details of her life and she certainly wasn't going to tell him she'd never had a boyfriend. It was too humiliating—and none of his business.

Daisy turned to face him and was surprised to find that he'd moved closer. Too close, she thought, as the scant foot that separated them shrank to six inches when he took another step toward her. "Umm," she stammered lamely. Her breasts tingled with awareness and need as she tried to remember what she'd been about to say. It was going to be something scathing, something that would put him in his place permanently.

"Snoring?" he prompted as he stared at her mouth, making her lick her lower lip self-consciously.

"Oh," she said finally. "Well, no one's ever mentioned it, anyway." A broad window that looked out over the Santa Margarita bay framed Alec's powerful body, silhouetting him against the brilliant hues of blue sky and ocean behind him. The view was gorgeous. She mentally claimed this room if they were forced to stay.

"Good," he said but his expression turned cloudy before he turned and stalked toward the common room. "Then I guess we'll have to take it. Let's just try to stay out of each other's way as much as possible."

Great. A three-month platonic slumber party with a man who's been starring in my erotic dreams for the past year. But instead she said to his retreating back, "I'm game if you are. And don't worry. After we have dinner with the Baldwins tonight, I'm going to go meet Troy and his friends so you'll have some time alone right from the get-go."

By the time he turned around—and it didn't take long—his expression had gone from merely cloudy to a full-blown storm. "You aren't serious."

"Sure I am," she said, although she hadn't given it much thought until he'd made that crack about staying out of each other's way. *The big jerk.* "I figure I'll be here for a few months. And I certainly don't want to impose on you for my social life." Even though she was pretending to examine the bedding, she chanced a glance at him through her lashes.

Uh-oh. Tornado warning.

"Fine," he said, his voice tight. She checked, but his posture and expression weren't transmitting *fine.* "But if you insist on going, I'm going with you."

Annoyance prickled along her spine. If there was one thing she didn't need, it was another big brother. And even if she did, Alec would not be on the short list of candidates. "No, thanks," she said. *If you come with me, I'll just want to be alone with you.* "I'd rather go by myself."

Exaggerated patience rang in his voice when he said, "Daisy, I'm responsible for you."

That sent her from merely annoyed to just plain mad in two seconds flat. What was it about her that made the men in her life treat her like she was a helpless child? More important, why couldn't this *particular* man see her as a woman? After all, there was no difference between her and any of his bimbo girlfriends, and she didn't see him following *them* around feeling burdened by responsibility.

"The *hell* you are, Alec," she said firmly. "I'm a grown woman, going to a party I was invited to by a friend."

"Hey," he said with a shrug and a tone that brooked no argument. "Your friend invited me, too. And I'm going."

Daisy had to bite her tongue—literally—to keep from telling him where he really *could* go. So rather than say something she'd surely regret, she swept passed him, stormed outside and grabbed Bam Bam's carrier and the remaining bags. When she returned, Alec was setting up his laptop on one of the large tables in what had just become their field office.

"The front bedroom is mine," she said, spoiling for another fight and wondering how he'd gotten so far under her skin so fast.

"Fine with me, but keep that cat in there. Cats and I don't get along."

"That's a shocker," she said with a sniff.

She banged her bags into a wall or two in her haste to leave the room, but still heard him call after her, "Dinner's in an hour."

"Right," she mumbled under her breath. "Like I'm the one who's late for everything."

"What?"

"Sure thing," she sang out with exaggerated sweetness. And with that, she closed her door firmly, threw her bags on the bed, freed her agitated cat and wondered how on earth she could still be pining for someone who could make her this mad.

Four

Dinner with the Baldwins turned out to be just the distraction Daisy needed. The only thing that kept it from being perfect was that Virginia had seated Alec so close to Daisy that their elbows touched constantly, so close that the warm, spicy scent of him constantly sent her mind wandering. So close, in fact, that the heat from his body made her feel like scootching her chair away from him so she wouldn't get burned.

But she didn't. She sat still, stayed focused on the conversation and forced herself to steal only sporadic glimpses of him out of the corner of her eye. He looked positively dishy in a dark-blue silk shirt and black pants. His mahogany hair was just unkempt enough to tempt her to drag her fingers through it. His smile and his laughter were quick and genuine.

She'd been out of her mind to take this job. They'd only

been here half a day and he was already driving her crazy. How was she going to handle ninety-odd more?

There was an up side, however, and it was that Daisy now found herself among friends. Joseph Baldwin was charming and witty, Virginia was a wonderful hostess, and their beautiful island home, perched high above the town of Paloma, was comfortable while still screaming style and sophistication. During a meal that had been prepared by the Baldwins' personal chef, their hosts gave them an entertaining history of Santa Margarita and spoke of their excitement at finally realizing their dream of restoring the old mansions.

"Are you sure I haven't told you this story already?" Virginia asked as the final course was served. When they assured her she hadn't, she went on with her story. "A long time ago, my father owned a movie studio. You may have heard of it. Cosmopolitan Pictures?"

Daisy and Alec both nodded. Everyone had heard of Cosmopolitan Pictures. The studio had made some of Daisy's favorite classic films.

"In the studio's heyday, my father bought up the majority of the land on this island so he would have a safe place for his most famous actors and actresses to come and vacation. That way he could keep an eye on them *and* keep their names out of the gossip columns."

She went on to explain how the island grew up around the seven mansions he'd built for his stable of stars to party in, how one particularly savvy and beautiful actress of the depression era, Paloma Estrella, had convinced him to build a casino and to bring in businesses like bars and grocery stores and laundries and motels. "And that was the start of the town of Paloma. It seemed only fair to him that the town be named after his inspiration."

"What an exciting childhood you must have had," Daisy said, smiling at the wistfulness on Virginia's face. "All those glamorous people."

"I'm afraid I was in boarding school most of the year, but the summers here with my mother and father were magical," she said with a smile that made her look years younger. "Watching those mansions slowly fall apart for the past thirty years has depressed me. That's one reason I'm so anxious to see them full of people and life and laughter again."

While they finished their dinner, Virginia explained that the properties had been tied up in the courts after Cosmopolitan Pictures was sold off, piece by piece, upon her father's death.

"In the end," Joseph said as a maid cleared away the last of the dishes, "the fact that the properties were under court protection is probably the only thing that kept them from being sold to a developer and torn down."

When the two couples moved to the terrace, Joseph and Virginia settled onto one overstuffed rattan love seat, leaving the other for Alec and Daisy. Alec waited for her to take a seat, but after eyeing the intimate space, she opted to stand at the terrace's railing to watch the activity on Paloma's dock and main street below. A moment later, Alec finally sat down and asked the Baldwins to tell him about the architect who had designed their beautiful hillside home.

Only a very few cars were permitted on the island at any one time, so golf carts were the transportation of choice. Most locals drove them, and visitors, like Daisy and Alec, usually used one provided by their hotel. The result of this

was that the town looked Lilliputian from her vantage point—
little white carts darted about and people honked their high-
pitched horns as they waited impatiently to maneuver into
miniature stalls in tiny parking lots. Daisy found it all vaguely
disorienting, as if she'd been transported to another dimen-
sion.

When the maid appeared with a cart laden with heavenly
smelling coffee and several trays of desserts, Daisy reluctantly sat down and tried not to notice the weight and warmth
of Alec's big, hunky body as he brushed up against her.

Breathe, she told herself. It'll all be over in a few months.
And still her skin flushed hotly as the pressure against her
thigh increased and her body responded to Alec's nearness in
that traitorous way it had almost since the first day she'd met
him.

"So, Alec," Virginia said as she passed a cup of coffee to
him. "I've been meaning to ask you. How's your mother?"

Daisy had taken countless messages from Alec's mother
over the years and spoken to her dozens of times. Barbara
Mackenzie had a rushed, clipped voice and a way of speaking that always reminded Daisy of someone who was hail-
ing a cab. Yet right at that moment, Daisy realized that she
didn't know anything else about Alec's mother—not even
what she looked like. Now that she thought about it, he didn't
have any family pictures in his office at all.

Alec hesitated slightly before passing a cup of coffee on
to Daisy. "Fine," he said at last. "I believe she's in Florence
at the moment."

"Oh, no. Last I heard," Virginia said as she opened a little
blue packet and stirred sweetener into her coffee, "she was
back in London appraising some of the royal family's jewelry."

"Is that right?" Alec asked, but not like it was a question. More like he didn't care in the least about his mother's whereabouts. "So tell me, Mrs. Baldwin—"

"Virginia," she interjected.

"Virginia," Alec said, nodding. "Tell me again how you know Barbara."

Daisy fumbled her tiny silver teaspoon onto her delicate china saucer. *Barbara?* He called his mother *Barbara?*

"Goodness, I can't even remember where we first met," Virginia said with a questioning glance at her husband. "One function or another. Possibly one of the auctions she organized for Sotheby's years ago. Before she started her own auction house."

Everyone had heard of Mackenzie Auctioneers, but until this moment, Daisy hadn't known it belonged to Alec's family. As Daisy swung her gaze back to Alec, she marveled at all the things she didn't know about this man who could make her go all breathless and fluttery just by sitting down next to her.

"And," Alec said with a forced casualness that Daisy recognized from many tense negotiations with contractors, "is that how you found out about my company?"

"I don't think so," Virginia said slowly, again looking to her husband for help in recalling a detail.

"I read about your work in a trade publication," Joseph said, coming to his wife's rescue. "As I remember it wasn't a very flattering piece, but the article's pictures told us what we wanted to know."

Alec felt the tension drain from his body as he thanked Joseph for the compliment. Until tonight he hadn't realized that the Baldwins knew who his mother was, let alone that they were all old pals from the damned neighborhood. The fact that they'd never mentioned it seemed strange, but the idea that he might owe this job not only to Daisy but to the mother he'd managed to completely avoid for the past few years was too sickening to contemplate.

A warm ocean breeze fluttered across the terrace, bringing with it what Alec was beginning to realize was the scent of Daisy Kincaid. Sweet like sugar, spicy like cinnamon, enticing like fresh-baked cookies, it brought a slow smile to his lips—which was strange since he really didn't feel like smiling at all.

That afternoon in the hotel room, he'd only meant to tease her when he'd asked whether any of her old boyfriends had told her she snored. But when her tongue had darted out to lick those sweet lips of hers, the concept of teasing had gone out the window. At that moment the thought of her with another man had made him mad as hell.

That's why he'd insisted on taking her to Troy's frigging party. That's why he was stuck with her for the rest of the night even though he kept telling himself he should stay far, far away from her. And that's why he was slowly but surely losing his grip—on both his priorities and his sanity.

He chanced a quick look at Daisy and saw the unmistakable glint of curiosity in her wide, dark eyes. The Baldwins were busy poring over a tray of desserts so he said, "What?" in a low voice.

"What was that all about?" she whispered fiercely.

"Nothing." He shrugged innocently, hoping she'd drop the idea of grilling him about his mother. Had he been that transparent or was Daisy doing that mind-reading thing she did so well?

Daisy looked like she was going to pursue it for a moment, then she glanced past him and put on a sweet expression for the Baldwins who had turned to offer them the tray.

Unfortunately, Alec was sure it was only a temporary reprieve. As he now knew, Daisy was a stubborn little thing. But what she didn't know about him was that she'd finally met her match.

The kegger was even worse than Alec had imagined. Hordes of tanned, healthy twenty- and thirty-somethings mingled on the small cottage's patio, each one clutching a brightly colored plastic cup foaming over with beer suds and yelling to be heard above the loud, grating music pouring from four enormous speakers. The men all wore shorts and flip-flops and the same Hawaiian shirts Alec had given to the Goodwill decades earlier. The women all wore tight skirts and skimpy tops and too much makeup. His first impression was that he'd either gone to hell or been tragically transported back to his USC undergrad days.

"Let's get a beer, Alec," Daisy yelled into his ear over the din.

He looked down to see that her eyes were bright, her expression eager. She'd left her glasses behind tonight and, without them, she looked younger, prettier and much, much more dangerous than he wanted to admit.

He sighed. Her inexplicable excitement about coming to this asinine clambake had at least made her forget about grilling him for more details about that conversation on the terrace. And for that he was grateful, so he yelled, "Okay," and guided her through the crowd with a gentle hand on the small of her back.

As they fought their way to the keg, the warmth of her body heated his palm and the silky fabric of her dress slid maddeningly across his fingertips. A low flame flared up, and in that moment he knew that he wanted nothing more than for all the people around them to disappear so he could be alone with Daisy Kincaid.

Suddenly the crowd on a tiny, makeshift dance floor surged toward them, running into them both and knocking them off balance. Daisy fell back against him, and he instinctively pulled her behind him to protect her—and then realized his mistake the moment the front of her body pressed up against the back of his.

Her curves burned where they touched him, her breath scorched where it skittered across his neck, her fingers branded him where they intertwined with his.

Damn.

As soon as the crowd had settled down, he stepped away from her, took her small, warm hand in his and rocketed toward the keg. She'd wanted to come to this party and he wasn't about to let her come alone. But now that they were here, he wasn't sure it was such a good idea. She'd been frying his brain all night with that slinky black dress and the seductive sway of her hips as she tottered around on those sexy heels. Hell, it'd been hard enough just sitting next to her at dinner. Now he was supposed to endure this, too?

Daisy frowned. She couldn't imagine what Alec was so upset about. After all, *she* was the one who'd just been unceremoniously yanked behind him like she was a bad child who'd wandered into a busy street. She was the one that had this dang crush that kept getting worse and worse even though she was supposed to be getting over it.

Beer sloshed over the rim of the yellow plastic tumbler Alec thrust into her hand. Then he glanced around the crowded patio as if searching for an escape route. "I'm going to go find the real bar," he shouted over the music. "Troy must've bought some of the hard stuff with that wad of cash I gave him this afternoon."

And then, just like that, she was alone.

She frowned at Alec's retreating back, then sternly reminded herself that she hadn't wanted him to come with her, anyway. This was exactly what she'd planned. It was just as well, she thought as she watched him disappear into the crowd. Yep, just as well.

She leaned against the railing that enclosed the patio and took a tiny sip of her beer. It was cold and thick and refreshing. As she licked a bit of foam off her top lip, she looked around at all the happy, tipsy, attractive people, then looked down at her own outfit. Her long black sleeveless dress and heeled sandals had been perfect for the Baldwins' dinner party, but here on Troy's patio she was definitely overdressed compared to all the bare-midriffed, short-skirted, smoky-eyed women all around her. Feeling out of place and nervous, Daisy took several big gulps of her beer in quick succession.

"Daisy!"

A tanned and handsome Troy came up beside her, one beer in each hand, his wide, white grin shining down on her with staggering wattage. "I'm so glad you're here. I didn't think your grouch of a boss was going to set you free for the night. Hey," he said before she could tell him Alec had come, too, "you look like you're ready for a refill."

Daisy started to object, then glanced at her cup and was surprised to see it was already empty. "Don't mind if I do," she said, plunking her empty yellow cup on the railing and taking a blue one from Troy. Alec really was a grouch. A grouch she couldn't seem to shake out of her fantasies, of course, but she was going to keep trying. "What a great party."

"Now that you're here it is. You wanna go get lost with me?" he asked, offering her his arm with a show of gallantry.

She smiled at his silly banter. Although he was probably a few years older than her own twenty-eight, he seemed younger and so full of life and energy that she couldn't help but enjoy his attention. "Absolutely," she said, taking a quick look around for Alec, the Incredible Disappearing Man. "Where're we going?" she asked as Troy began to pull her toward the house.

"The Cave," he said mysteriously and let out a horror-film cackle.

The Cave turned out to be another patio that was accessed by walking all the way through the house and out another set of doors. The Cave was hopping, and for the next hour or so, Daisy learned how to play a couple of drinking games. Because she'd had to work to put herself through college, she'd always been too busy—and later, too old—to socialize with her fellow students. Tonight, a dozen of her new best friends were doing their best to remedy that.

When someone broke out the supplies to make something called an "inverted margarita," Daisy took a break and went to find the ladies' room. The party was in full swing, so she had to wait in line for ten minutes before she got her turn, then before she went back to the Cave, she took a quick look around for Alec.

He wasn't hard to find. He was on the front patio, doing what he did best. There he was, looking ultramasculine and confident, leaning against a wall talking to a tall, gorgeous, blond bimbo.

Daisy almost choked on a potent cocktail of anger and self-doubt. That was her problem right there, all wrapped up in a tiny tropical-print sarong. Maybe if I were more like that, she thought, Alec would've seen me as a woman. Not that she could get taller or blonder or curvier. Just *sexier*…and maybe a little more self-assured.

That's it, she told herself, and wondered why the patio seemed to suddenly spin a little. *I've cracked the code.* Bold, confident, sexy. If she could somehow pull it off, men would slobber at her feet, just like Alec was doing with that flashy blonde right that very minute. I'll do it, she vowed silently, the very next time I have the opportunity.

Which should be sometime before the next ice age.

The blonde moved her perfect body up against Alec's side. He smiled down at his conquest, snapping Daisy out of her reverie. Typical, she thought as she pasted on a smile and headed back into the house. It was exactly what she needed to remember that once this job was complete, Alec was off her Christmas card list forever.

Alec caught the twinkle of Daisy's silver hoop earrings as she turned and sauntered away on those sexy, strappy heels. For the past hour, Alec had been battling with himself, wavering between going to look for her and keeping a safe distance from her. And he'd just about decided that he needed to go find her when she'd appeared on the patio for a moment, then disappeared just as quickly. He wondered for the dozenth time where she'd been for the last hour and if she'd been with Troy. Then he ground his teeth and wondered why he cared so much.

"So what's it going to be?" a soft, feminine voice purred from beside him.

Startled, he looked down to see the overly done-up blonde

gazing at him. He'd been so busy watching Daisy, he'd almost forgotten about her. And that, he thought with a frown, wasn't like him at all.

"What's what going to be, darlin'?" he asked as he glanced back at the doorway where Daisy had just vanished.

"This is definitely going to happen," she murmured in his ear as she placed one manicured hand on his chest. "But I'm sharing a hotel room with a bunch of girlfriends. It'll have to be your place."

"Unfortunately," he said as he tore his gaze away from the doorway and looked back down at the beautiful woman at his side, "I don't think that my roommate would approve. I'll just have to take a rain check."

He blinked. Had he really just said that? Clearly, he thought as he removed the blonde's hand from his shirt with a shadow of regret, his mind was so preoccupied with Daisy, his natural instincts were failing him. But even so, in the time it took him to walk across the patio, he'd practically forgotten all about the woman, her offer and the rain check. He was much more interested in making sure Troy wasn't doing something that Alec wouldn't approve of—which would be just about anything that had to do with Daisy.

It didn't take long to scan the small cottage. Daisy was nowhere to be found, so Alec stalked out the back door to a smaller patio which was dimly lit by long strings of white Christmas lights. It was easy enough to find her there, all right, but the sight that lay before him made him so mad he had to force himself to breathe.

She was perched at the edge of an old redwood bench, her dress hiked dangerously up to midthigh, her tall heels making her legs look absurdly long. And good old Troy was kneeling at her feet, caressing that graceful stem of a leg.

He had to hand it to the guy. He was fast. But as Alec covered the distance across the patio, he made some quick plans to slow Troy down permanently.

Daisy's head snapped up as he approached them. "Alec!" she said, her voice unmistakably higher and brighter than it should be.

"Hey, man," Troy said as he dropped the hem of her dress and stood up. "I didn't know you were here," he began with a smile.

"I'm sure you didn't." Alec stared at Troy until his smile died. "Time to go, Daisy," Alec said with what he thought was remarkable calm as he clenched and unclenched his hands at his sides. When she didn't get up, he looked over to see her chin set stubbornly, her cheeks flushed, her eyes sparkling with an unfamiliar light.

She set a blue tumbler down on the bench beside her with great care even though it appeared to be empty. Alec saw more empty cups scattered about the immediate vicinity, and it gave him a clue as to why her voice was slightly slurred when she said, "Don't be silly. I'm not ready to go yet."

"Yes, you are." Considering that he wanted to slug Troy and sling Daisy over his shoulder and take her away from here as fast as he could, Alec was proud of how reasonable he was being.

"But, dude," Troy said cheerfully. "The night's yet young. Let's go get another drink and—"

"No, thanks. We've stayed too long already." Alec took Daisy's hand and pulled her to her feet. "We have to go."

She stood there a moment, looking from Alec to Troy and back again. Then she looked down at her small hand

enclosed in Alec's larger one, and no one was more surprised than he was when he gave her a light, encouraging
squeeze.

She looked up at him, and a sweet, simple smile curved
her lips before she said, "Oh, all right. You win."

"Okay," Troy said genially. "But if you change your minds,
we'll be raging all night here. Thanks for coming by," he said,
and gave Daisy a look that made Alec want to put a fist
through his big, toothy grin.

"Our pleasure," Daisy began, but Alec had had enough.
Still holding Daisy's hand, he turned and tugged against her
resistance until he felt her follow him.

As they made their way back to the main patio, Alec wondered what the hell was happening to the dependable, no-nonsense, bespectacled Daisy he knew—and what the hell was
making him feel so protective? Nothing would make him happier than to chalk it up to a brotherly instinct, but since his
thoughts about the all-new Daisy Kincaid were far from fra-
ternal, that wouldn't wash. But still, something about her
was getting to him. So much so that he hadn't snapped up that
blond, willing, young thing who even now was doing everything she could to catch his eye as he sped across the patio
with Daisy in tow.

Whatever it was, he thought as they hit the sidewalk and
the music receded behind them, he definitely did not like
it.

"What," Daisy said, stopping in her tracks mulishly and
bringing them to a dead halt, "is your problem?"

"I'm not the one with a problem, my little St. Pauli Girl.
You're the one with a problem."

"St. Pauli Girl?" She lifted her cute little snoot into the air and pulled her hand from his. "If you're referring to the tiny glass of beer I had tonight—"

"Tiny glass? I saw your little cup collection."

She planted her fists on her hourglassy hips. "What were you doing? Counting my drinks?"

"It was pretty hard to miss."

She shook her head dismissively. "So what? A few of glasses of beer makes me the queen of the beer garden?"

"We were there for an hour, Daisy."

This seemed to stump her momentarily, but she recovered. "Well, that doesn't give you the right to haul me out of there like you were on some sort of rescue mission," she said, her voice rising as she warmed to her topic. "I didn't need rescuing, thank you."

"It sure looked like you did. I'm no Puritan, but I think a twelve-hour acquaintance isn't quite long enough for Troy to be shaving your legs."

Daisy looked at him like he'd lost his mind. "Shaving my—" she sputtered. "I spilled some beer. Troy was just being chivalrous by drying my leg off with his shirt."

"Uh-huh," Alec said, his anger rising again as he remembered the sight of Daisy and Troy on the patio. "Sounds like a real gentleman."

She cocked her head to the side, and her curls spilled gracefully over one shoulder. Until this week, Daisy had worn her hair in a tight twist every single day. This week, for some reason, she'd decided to let her dark, shiny, chestnut curls down. It was driving him nuts.

And just like that, an image flashed through Alec's mind unbidden, an image of him burying his fingers in her hair, tipping her head back and kissing her until she—

"You know what your problem is, Alec?" she demanded, wrenching him from his thoughts. "You don't trust anybody. And that's just sad."

"Of course I trust people," he answered quickly, but knew in the very moment he said it that he'd be hard-pressed to name anyone if pushed to do so.

"Liar. And your suspicious nature ruined my plan for tonight."

"You had a plan?"

"Yes, I did, and no thanks to you…." She tipped her head to the other side, considering him with an expression that made him uneasy.

As he waited for her to come clean with her big plan, he tried not to notice the glint of her earrings as they reflected the lights of the harbor behind him or the press of her breasts against the dark fabric of her dress or the way she tugged at her lower lip with her teeth as she regarded him.

"Ah, what the hell," she said, taking a step closer. "I'm going to Plan B."

And with that, she went up on her toes, placed her fingertips on his shoulders and gently touched her soft, warm lips to his.

Five

Their lips met in a tangle of what Alec knew with a rush of clarity was pent-up anticipation, and that knowledge sent a bolt of desire ripping through him that shocked him right down to his shoelaces.

He wanted to pull her closer, taste her sweetness, take control but something told him to hold back, so he merely let his mouth follow hers down the warm, inviting path of least resistance—and let his hands blaze a trail of their own. Both palms skimmed Daisy's narrow waist and stroked the fine muscles of her back before he pushed one hand into that tempting mass of curly hair and the other slipped lower and pulled her against the terrible pressure that was growing with each soft breath she exhaled against his lips.

It was, he realized, just like he'd been imagining it would be.

After all the years they'd worked side by side, when had he

begun to daydream about this? he wondered with a vague sense of surprise. Could it have been since the beginning? Since that very first day when she'd come into his office with the quickest, sweetest laugh he'd ever heard? But then Daisy's lips parted beneath his, and the tempting mystery of her opened up to him and he forgot about everything but the woman in his arms.

At the first coy slide of her warm, wet tongue against his, the desire he'd felt earlier settled solidly, achingly low in his belly. The weight of it made him deepen the kiss, made him tighten his hold on her, made his mouth slanting against hers feel almost desperate. Her sweet scent mingled with the cool, damp ocean air around them, a heady combination that intensified as her curvy little body crowded closer and her soft breasts pressed up against his chest and stole his breath away.

Their tongues began to wage a sweet battle for control as her breath fanned lightly against his cheek and the tiniest of moans slipped from between her lips. The soft noise rippled through him and he felt his control slipping, felt himself being pushed to a limit he didn't even know he had and—

C-r-a-s-h!

The unmistakable sound of shattering glass and the laughter of a group of partygoers spilling out onto the sidewalk behind them was enough to pull Alec from his haze, enough to remind him that Daisy, too, had been drinking tonight. He pulled away from her, dropped his hands to his sides and took a half step back. For God's sake, if he didn't put a stop to this, there was no doubt they'd end up in bed together. And even though that sounded like a spectacular plan right now, he knew Daisy. Tonight she might be acting like she wanted this, but tomorrow she would regret it.

The sounds of the party grew louder as his mind grew

clearer. The space where his brain used to be was still fogged by desire and his body still pulsed with need, but as he slowly became aware of the sweet, yeasty smell of the beer that clung to Daisy, he realized that if he'd taken advantage of her state of drunkenness, he would've been the biggest chump in history.

Before he spoke, he looked down into her pretty, dark-eyed gaze and saw desire smoldering there—the same desire that he knew was still burning inside him. He swallowed hard and clenched his fists to keep himself from pulling her right back up against him.

"Daisy," he said quietly, "that was a bad idea." Dammit, had he really just heard his voice crack?

"It was?" Her tempting, kiss-swollen lips curved into a tipsy smile. "Why?"

It *was* a bad idea, he told himself again as he stared down into her lovely velvet-brown eyes. She'd had too much to drink. He was her boss. They had a job to do. They were stuck on this island together for three months. And she wasn't even his type.

At least she didn't used to be.

"For one thing," he said, "you're drunk."

For a moment she was silent, as if considering his claim. Then she smiled and weaved toward him a little, reaching out at the last moment to brace her hands against his chest. "Yes. You're right."

He almost groaned as she let her hands slip seductively down his chest, curving her fingertips into his stomach muscles on the way down. "That's it," he ground out as he grabbed her wrists and pinned her arms down to her sides.

"Oh, c'mon." Daisy pouted. "Don't be a killjoy."

She was a good pouter. Adorable, in fact. Her lips formed a perfect bow, her eyes begged him to let her have her way and she thrust one hip out so sweetly he almost wanted to give her what she wanted. But he couldn't. Not tonight.

Tonight it was his misfortune to be the sane and sober one for both of their sakes.

"Daisy," he said as he set her away from him. "I may not be a gentleman in all cases, but even I won't stoop this low."

The words hit her gradually, but they had an impact far beyond what he'd intended. He felt like a bully as he watched the confusion gather in her eyes, as her silly smile dissolved, as her body straightened and she crossed her arms loosely beneath the breasts he was now longing to touch.

Stop it, Mackenzie.

"Fine," she said, and there was an unmistakable tinge of hurt in her voice as she turned and headed in the wrong direction. "We should go then."

With a sigh, Alec followed her, reaching her in three long strides. "I appreciate your cooperation," he said as he put an arm around her shoulder and steered her in a half circle, "but our cart is this way."

She sagged against him as they walked, and he gritted his teeth at the sensation of her body slipping relentlessly along his from shoulder to hip. Their fit, he noticed grimly, was absolutely perfect.

Alec helped her climb unsteadily into the cart, then drove home as fast as that stupid electric engine would take them. His mission? To get her safely into bed—alone—so he could start to formulate the perfect speech for tomorrow morning. Of course, he had no idea what he was going to say. How could he when he didn't even know what he wanted?

He glanced over at Daisy and wondered what she was thinking behind all that silence. She was probably a little embarrassed, which would be a totally understandable reaction. After all, if she'd been sober, she'd never have kissed him that way. It just wasn't her style to do such a thing on a dark sidewalk with him. She was too levelheaded, too sweet, too nice and smart for that—and for him.

"I've never been much of a drinker," Daisy said defiantly as she waited for Alec to open the door to their suite.

"Really?" He tried—and failed miserably—to keep the amusement out of his tone.

Luckily she was pretty looped, so she didn't notice. "It's true," she said, and brushed past him to enter the room.

He flipped on the light as her heels click-clacked across the tile floor, then he closed the door and turned around just in time to see her perfect little behind in its tight black wrapper headed straight for his room.

"Whoa, whoa. Hold it right there." He came up behind her, put both hands on her shoulders and steered her toward her own room. Feeling as he did right now, having her anywhere near his bed would definitely strain his chivalry to the breaking point.

She sat down on her bed with a plop, causing her cat to leap to the floor in a fit of hissing, its displeasure at being woken up evident.

"Sorry," she said, but so quietly he had to strain to hear her. She fell back against the pillows, curled up and closed her eyes. "I didn't mean to scare you away."

Alec tugged off her sandals one at a time and thought about helping her undress but immediately discarded the idea as too dangerous. She looked so pretty, her hair splayed over the pillow, her hand curled next to her face, the barest of smiles on her lips.

Lord help him, he was attracted to her even now. He had to get the hell out of there, so he pulled the blanket over her and headed for the door. Seconds later, the cat jumped back up on the bed, shot Alec a reproachful glare, curled himself up next to Daisy and fell instantly asleep.

Too bad Alec wasn't going to be nodding off that easily tonight. Not with the memory of Daisy in his arms, not with the feel of her lips and the pressure her body permanently tattooed on his mind.

As he turned off the light and closed her door quietly, he thought about the words she'd mumbled just before she'd fallen asleep. And although he knew she'd meant them for her disgruntled cat, they could've easily applied to him. She *had* scared him—and in a way he'd never been before in his life.

Because for the first time, Alec Mackenzie was attracted to a woman who made him smile, who made him think and who made him want to be a different kind of man.

Daisy didn't want to wake up, but eventually the roar of Bam Bam's normally soothing purr forced her to crack an eye open. Then she immediately pulled a pillow over her face to drown out both the noise and the hideous amount of sunlight pouring into her room.

"Why do I feel so awful?" she mumbled to Bam Bam from beneath the pillow. "Surely those two glasses of wine at dinner didn't…"

As the memories trickled in, her stomach sank. *Ohmigosh.* She sat straight up in bed, then cursed because the sudden movement made her head pound even harder.

She'd thrown herself at Alec—and he'd thrown her right back.

A strange sense of unreality fell over her, making her wonder for a moment if she'd really done what she thought she'd done. But she had only to close her eyes to find the answer. She could still feel the sensations of the silken pressure of his lips, the delicious slide of his tongue, the rough texture of his skin under her fingertips. Oh, yes, she thought with a pained groan. Yes, she had indeed kissed Alec, thoroughly and completely. And it had been better than all her many imaginings had prepared her for.

As she swung her legs around and touched her bare feet to the cool tile floor, her memories of the party flowed back unrelentingly. She remembered her decision to, at the very next opportunity, be brazen and sexy like one of Alec's bimbos. She remembered her careless consumption of beer and her wholehearted participation in all those drinking games. She even vaguely remembered her foolish decision to put it all on the line once and for all and kiss Alec. And then she remembered the cherry on top of her humiliation sundae: his firm rejection and his pronouncement that being with her would be "stooping too low."

She let her heavy, throbbing head fall into her waiting hands. Daisy had always had an active imagination. Over the past year or so, she'd created hundreds of short films in her mind that depicted—some in graphic detail—how an intimate encounter with Alec would go. But not one of them had ended with him telling her in no uncertain terms that she was so unappealing to him that he couldn't possibly lower himself to be with her.

Daisy got up, swayed a little, then began to pace the room slowly in her bare feet. Ever since she'd met him, Alec had been plowing through women like a wheat harvester. She'd put dozens of his bimbos' names into her Rolodex, only to pull and chuck each card in a matter of weeks. It was his pattern. Tried and true.

She pulled back the curtains and winced as more bruising light flooded the room. So what in the hell was wrong with *her?* Was she so repellent, so unpleasant and unattractive that he couldn't even bring himself to have a *meaningless fling* with her?

Apparently, the answer was yes.

Her anger flared and continued to blaze hotly, making her embarrassment and hurt feelings dim by comparison.

This was it. What had happened last night really was the last log she would ever allow Alec to toss into the fire that had finally succeeded in burning her self-respect to a cinder. After all, he couldn't possibly make his feelings about her any more clear. Sure, he'd said he needed her during their showdown in her kitchen, but that was in a work sense *and nothing more.* Last night had proved that, hadn't it?

And although she'd said it before, she knew right down to her bones that this time it was different. This time, she promised herself as she stalked to the bathroom and twisted on the shower's hot water valve, her crush was truly extinguished. Never again would she risk her heart that way. Not with Alec.

No matter what.

Alec heard Daisy before he saw her.

She was laughing, and the familiar, comforting sound of it rippled through him, making him smile in spite of his dark mood. When he opened the door, he saw that she was talking on the phone in the suite's kitchenette, the receiver pressed between her shoulder and ear as she reached up to put something into one of the cabinets.

While he'd visited the job sites this morning, he'd spent a considerable amount of energy convincing himself that what had happened between them was a fluke. In fact, until this moment, he'd been almost positive that his attraction to her would seem silly in the light of day. But that wasn't exactly what happened.

What happened was that he was frozen in place as he took in the enticing length of her—from her tanned, toned calves that flexed as she tipped up onto her toes, to her lovely behind encased in khaki shorts, to her light-green top stretched tight over her finely muscled back and shoulders. He shoved his hands into his pockets and willed the damnable tightness in his groin to melt away before she turned around and caught him staring.

"I miss you, too, Tom," she said in a fond voice as she took more groceries out of the bags on the counter.

His head snapped up. *Tom?* She missed someone named *Tom?* he thought with a frown. *Who the hell was Tom?*

"Well, you can always come out here. By boat, I'm just two hours away." She paused, then laughed again. "That's right. It's just that you're such a hunk," she said as she leaned over and put something under the sink, "that I forgot you get seasick."

So Daisy's Tom was a hunk who couldn't hold down his cookies on a little boat ride? Alec thought as he tried not to admire her exceptional backside. If Tom was as big a wuss about flying, it would effectively eliminate him as competition—at least for the next few months.

Alec blinked. He was tired, but not that tired. After a sleepless night and half a day thinking about it, hadn't he'd already decided that he was going to put a stop to this…this *thing* that was brewing between him and Daisy? There *was* something brewing, he couldn't deny that any longer. But he also couldn't deny that she was all wrong for him. Dead wrong.

She was the kind of woman a man brought home to meet the parents, the kind of woman who made a man willing to talk about kitchen remodels and the thread count of his sheets, the kind of woman who inspired a man to start thinking about forever.

In short, she was exactly the kind of woman he'd been avoiding all his adult life.

He must have made some kind of noise because Daisy turned around, and when she saw him her smile faded and her laughter turned into a small choking sound. She leaned back against the counter and gripped the receiver tight enough to make her fingers turn white. "I have to go," she said into the phone, never taking her eyes off him. "The boss is back."

The boss.

She'd said the words flatly, putting a distance between them that he'd never felt before. In that moment he knew last night had changed everything. Never again could they be just two people who liked each other and worked well together. Not now that he knew what she tasted like, what she felt like in his arms, what sweet, murmured sounds she made when they were so close he couldn't tell where she ended and he began.

Unfortunately, he thought as he struggled to scatter the images that were popping into his mind, he couldn't let anything happen. Among other things, she was the settling-down type and he really, *really* wasn't. He was a rat in rat's clothing, pretending to be nothing else but a man who liked to have a good time until the good times ended. It was all he was capable of and he'd always known it.

No, the thing to do here, he thought with a lingering sense of regret, was to try to keep a professional distance. The only thing he wondered now was if she was thinking the same thing.

"Hello, Alec," she said stiffly as she hung up the phone.

Okay, she was thinking the same thing. "Hello, Daisy," he said, and knew he was flirting with disaster as he walked toward the small kitchen. "Did you sleep well?"

A light flush spread across the smooth skin of her cheeks. "Like the dead, but I guess you already knew that considering the, uh, *state* I was in when you poured me into bed." She looked down at the floor. "I apologize for that, by the way."

"No need. Happens to the best of us." He reached past her to close a cabinet door she'd left open, then caught a whiff of the enticing fragrance he'd come to think of as Eau de Daisy.

Uh-oh.

For a moment it seemed like they'd both stopped breathing. He knew right then that if he didn't move away, he wasn't going to be able to resist kissing her—and he also knew that kissing her would definitely mess up that whole "professional distance" thing he'd just cooked up.

But he couldn't seem to move.

All he could think about was feeling her soft skin beneath his hands, of tasting her again, of hearing her make that little sound of pleasure he'd heard last night. He turned his head toward her and knew he was a fool and then…

She stepped gracefully away and left the kitchen and didn't stop until she was standing behind one of the large oak tables in the main room. "All our office stuff came today. I've almost got the computers hooked up," she said brightly.

Alec took a deep breath and leaned back against the edge of the counter she'd just abandoned and managed to say, "That's good," as he took a long look at her. Her eyes were downcast, her dark hair was tumbling over her shoulders in a curtain of curls, and even from that distance he could see that her hands trembled slightly as she slipped on her glasses.

Sunlight poured into the room through the French doors, and Alec watched as dust motes floated around in the beam of bright light that spread across the table in front of Daisy. And that's when he noticed for the first time that the furniture had been reorganized. Instead of being side by side, two of the tables faced each other from across the broad expanse of room and the third was set up smack in the center of them.

"Who moved the furniture?" he asked.

Daisy didn't look up. She was far too busy scooting her office supplies around on the tabletop. "I did."

For some reason it irritated him that she clearly wanted as much physical distance between them as possible. And the simple fact that she was acting like he suddenly had the plague made him want to bait her when the smart thing to do would be to just let things lie. "Are we going to install an intercom so we can talk to each other?"

She looked up, her dark eyes full of fire. "I thought you'd enjoy a little privacy for your phone calls."

"Hmm," he said as he walked toward her, never taking his eyes off her. "What if I don't want any privacy?"

"Well, maybe," she said, and he saw the light in her eyes flicker a bit, "maybe I want some privacy, then."

When he reached her desk, he put his hands down in the center of it and leaned forward until he was so close, he could see her pulse pounding at her throat and feel her warm, sweet breath on his face. Danger signals went off in his head, loud and insistent, but he ignored them. "So you can talk to Tom?"

Predictably, she blushed a deeper shade of pink. He'd never noticed how damn cute that blush was. "Tom or…whoever," she said, then changed the subject abruptly. "Everything should be working now except our Internet connection. Bill and I should have that fixed by the time we start work Monday morning."

"Who's Bill?" *And who's Tom? And, Lord, why do I care so much?*

"You know him. He's the desk clerk here. And he also works for the island's freight delivery company." She smiled a bit, apparently forgetting to be mad at him for the moment. "Did you know everyone on this island holds down a couple of jobs? Even the local pastor works at the grocery store during the week and—"

"Would you like to have dinner tonight?"

Her smile flat-lined as she lowered herself into her chair and stared at him in silence. In truth, he couldn't believe he'd asked her, either. Not when he'd just decided to minimize their contact to keep from making a mistake he'd regret.

"With you?" she asked, her voice tinged with skepticism.

"Of course, with me. Who else would I mean?"

"I don't know. Sometimes you…" She shook her head and opened up her laptop. "Never mind. I don't want to have dinner with you." Then she started to tap away on her keyboard like a woodpecker.

Let it go, he thought as he straightened and gazed down

at her. *It's for the best.* But then his curiosity—or was it pride?—got the better of him so he asked, "Why?"

Tappity-tap-tap. "Because."

He smiled. "Care to elaborate?"

Tappity-tappity-tap. "I have plans."

"I see," he said, and resisted asking what he really wanted to know. *Where? With who? And when will you be back?* Lord, he was losing his mind.

She stopped typing long enough to glance at her watch. "I'm sorry, Alec. I have to go."

He glanced at the clock on the wall, noted that it was two o'clock, then asked the question he had no right to ask. "When will you be back?"

"You sure are nosy today," she said as she gathered up her things.

"And you sure are mysterious."

When she opened the front door, the clanging of the harbor's buoys slipped into the room. "Let's just say you shouldn't wait up. Have a nice night, Alec."

Alec frowned. How was he supposed to have a nice night when she was going to be out God-knew-where with God-knew-who until God-knew-when? And how was he supposed to have a nice night when he was all alone with his realization that what he really wanted was to be with her?

"You, too," he called out as the door closed behind her. But anybody with a decent sense of hearing should have been able to tell that he didn't really mean it at all.

Six

Daisy could still hear the tone of Alec's husky, sexy voice as she pushed away her half-eaten sandwich and smiled at her lunch date, Virginia Baldwin.

"Anyway," Daisy said with a shrug, "I don't think I'm cut out for the whole dating game. I guess I just never developed any of those girly-girl qualities I would need to be good at it."

Virginia reached out across the red-checked table and patted Daisy's hand. "Small wonder, considering you lost your mother so young. I'm sure your father did his best," she added. "But there's no way anyone could expect him to have taught you all the things you needed to know."

Daisy smiled at the older woman and fiddled with her iced tea, a little embarrassed that she'd unloaded so much on Virginia who was, after all, a Mackenzie client. The thing was, though, for Daisy, Virginia had already become much more than a client. She was more like a kindly old aunt—although Daisy had still been careful to leave out all the little details concerning Alec when she'd confided that she was in a bit of funk today.

"Sometimes it feels like I'm invisible to the opposite sex," Daisy said. "Which is probably because I look like a librarian." She smiled as she pushed her reading glasses further up her nose. "But it doesn't make any difference. Even if I looked like a pinup girl, everything I know about meeting and attracting a man could almost fill a Dixie cup."

And last night had only served to prove that all over again.

"There's nothing wrong with how you look," Virginia said as she reached out impulsively and tucked a curl behind Daisy's ear.

The gesture reminded Daisy so much of her own mother, she went all soft inside. "I'm sorry, Virginia. We were getting together to talk about the project, and here I've been yammering—"

"Not at all," the older woman said with a wave of her bejeweled hand. "I wanted to spend some time with you and that's exactly what we're doing. Now," she said as she chewed on one perfect, oval fingernail and looked at Daisy appraisingly, "I have an idea."

Something about the gleam in Virginia's eye made Daisy a little uneasy. "An idea about the project?"

"No, no," she said as she gestured to the waitress and scribbled in the air with an invisible pen. "An idea for you. What you need is a good old-fashioned makeover. Hair, makeup, manicure. The works. And we've got some wonderful designer boutiques on Bayside Avenue, so we can give your closet a makeover, too," she said as she signed the bill with a flourish. "In one afternoon, we'll banish your blues and give you the confidence boost you obviously need to see how irresistible you are."

"Oh, I don't think—" Daisy began, but stopped in mid-protest. How great would it be to feel honest-to-God feminine for once in her life? Wouldn't it be empowering to have men twist their necks around to look at her as she walked by? And wouldn't it be thrilling to feel as though she had what it took to be a woman who was pursued by men?

The answer to all of those was a resounding yes. Plus, there was a tiny seed of evil in her that wanted Alec to see that beneath this capable, practical, unremarkable exterior there had always been a bimbo-in-training. If only he'd known.

Filled with an energy borne of new purpose, Daisy took off her glasses and smiled at her friend. "Let's do it."

Walking in heels like these was strictly a job for professionals, Daisy concluded as she picked her way down the pockmarked sidewalk, her hands full of shopping bags acquired during an afternoon spent in Paloma's finest shops. She looked down in an effort to keep from tipping over like a top-heavy doll, saw her toes, and was shocked all over again when she saw that her toenails were painted that bright, bright crimson that Virginia's manicurist had said was called Matador Red before she'd trilled *ay-ay-ay* like a flamenco dancer and applied it.

But a pedicure wasn't all Daisy had done.

At the urging of Virginia—and courtesy of the dozens of cell phone calls her friend had made to manicurists, hair-

dressers, dress shops, shoe stores and an establishment that
made Victoria's Secret look like they sold granny gowns—
Daisy had done it all. And all of it, right down to the last lipstick, had been Virginia's treat. Daisy smiled when she
remembered Virginia waving away her protests, saying, "I've
always wished I had a daughter I could spoil rotten. Now I
feel like I do."

The sun was long gone from the streets of Paloma, and the
evening crowds were starting to emerge from hotels and
houses and boats to make their way toward restaurants and
bars and cafés. Daisy looked to her left and caught a glimpse
of herself in the window of a dimly lit bar and had to remind
herself again that what she saw really was her own reflection.

Her heels were very trendy, strappy and high. Her silky,
light-blue skirt was tiny but gorgeous and exposed her legs
to midthigh, making them look so long she almost didn't
recognize them as her own. A sleeveless cashmere shell in the
same color as the skirt fit her like a glove except that it was
pulled tight across her normally normal-size breasts, which
had been increased by one size courtesy of her new lingerie.

Daisy stopped to peer in the window and touched her hair
self-consciously. It was still dark, still curly, but now it had
a certain unkempt, just-rolled-out-of-bed look that made her
feel like she should yank a brush through it to bring it under
control. And the salon had provided not only a manicurist and
a hairstylist, but a makeup artist who'd done a perfect but subtle job. Of course, when she tried to do it herself with all the
same products tomorrow, she'd probably end up looking like
Howdy Doody. But so what? Even if it was only for just one
night, feeling like Cinderella for a while was worth it.

A quick glance at the huge clock mounted atop the main

mast of a ship-shaped restaurant called *Pitcairn* was all it took to let her know her makeover had taken much longer than she'd anticipated. Maybe she could just grab a bite to eat here, she thought as she eyed a couple emerging from the restaurant hand in hand. She hated eating alone, but she was starving. And it wasn't as if she had plans or anything, in spite of what she'd told Alec earlier. Another white lie—but hey, at the time she'd have said almost anything to get out of having to sit across the table from him all night and pretend she wasn't still suffering from a terminal case of puppy love.

Daisy's stomach growled. Oh, what the hell, she thought and then she slipped inside and asked for a table for one.

She ignored the snotty look the barely legal hostess cast her way and followed the girl's chirpy little voice when she said over her shoulder, "Follow me, ma'am."

Ma'am? Good heavens, did she really look that old? A little deflated by the thought, Daisy nevertheless followed in the girl's wake and took a seat at a small table, dropping her bags on the floor as she did.

"Enjoy your dinner," the teenager said with syrup in her tone before she flounced away.

Daisy smoothed the napkin over her lap as she took in the restaurant's Polynesian theme. From the bamboo chairs to the lush foliage to the sarongs on the waitresses, this place had South Seas written all over it. She twisted around in her chair and moved a heavy branch of a rubber plant to get a better look at the unusual sunken bar…and looked right into Alec's amused gaze.

"Big plans, huh?" he asked, grinning like the devil.

Her heart hammered in her chest as her body went simultaneously hot and cold. "My plans are for after dinner," she lied, then let the branch snap back into place and turned around. She must be jinxed. There was no other explanation for how the last person she wanted to see in the world had been seated two feet away from her.

The plant rustled behind her. "Are your after dinner plans as exciting as your dinner plans?"

Daisy closed her eyes and counted to ten. When she got to fifteen, she turned around and smiled into his handsome face and his gorgeous indigo eyes. "I'll tell you all about it when I get home in the morning. How's that?"

If she'd expected a snappy response, she didn't get it. Instead, his eyes darkened as they roamed over her face, then his inspection moved southward where he lingered briefly on the deep vee of her cashmere sweater. When he looked up into her eyes again, his amusement was history.

"My God," he said finally. "What did you do?"

Embarrassment flared first, followed quickly by anger. Like the naïve fool that she was, she'd thought for one heady moment that he might notice the changes she'd made today and give her an actual compliment. "Thanks a lot, Alec," she said tersely and turned back around.

"No, no," she heard him protest from behind the heavy rubber plant. "You just…" She heard him sigh, heard his chair scrape against the worn hardwood floors, then she flushed hotly when he appeared beside her table.

Of its own volition, her hand went to her hair to smooth it. But she needn't have bothered because he wasn't looking at her hair. He was giving her a once over so thorough it sent her blood zooming through her from fingertips to toes.

"You look great," he said when his gaze returned to her face. "Really, really amazing."

"Right," she scoffed and opened up the menu to hide her face which was burning with a spicy brew of resentment and mortification.

Another chair scraped and she snuck a peek just in time to see Alec taking a seat across from her. The tip of his index finger appeared at the top of her menu and he lowered it until he could see her clearly. "Looks like you had a busy afternoon," he said with smile she couldn't quite read.

"Well, it takes time to turn a sow's ear into a silk purse." She didn't even try to keep the sarcasm out of her voice.

"I already told you I thought you looked great," he said and reached for the wine list the hostess had left behind. "Stop fishing."

Maybe she was fishing, she thought as she pretended to read the menu. And so what? Even though she didn't want anything from Alec anymore, didn't she deserve a few compliments after years of feeling like just another Doric column at Mackenzie Architectural?

"I don't remember asking you to join me," she said, feeling cranky and wanting to take it out on him.

"You didn't have to. I knew you wanted me to sit here."

"Oh? And how did you know that?"

He shot her a serene smile. "I could tell by the way you were playing hard to get."

She bit back a scathing response when she saw the waitress approaching. The woman looked so familiar, Daisy found herself squinting in the dim light to try to place her. Daisy was saved the trouble, though, when the woman smiled broadly and said, "Hey, hi! You're Mrs. Baldwin's friend. I see you've got one of your new outfits on."

Ah, the dress shop. "Yes, I do," Daisy said, and when Alec

looked up, his eyes filled with interest, she smoothed the soft cashmere against her stomach self-consciously. "Thanks again for your help today."

"My pleasure," the salesclerk/waitress said. "Did you know Mrs. Baldwin is here, too?" She gestured toward the front of the restaurant. "Right over there with that handsome husband of hers. But I see you've got that covered, too." She gave a not-so-discreet little jerk of her head in Alec's direction.

A little shiver of pleasure wiggled up Daisy's spine at the thought of being able to call him her one and only. Then reality crept back in. "He's not my husband," she told the woman. "He's my boss."

"Lucky you," the waitress said, shooting Alec an appreciative glance.

In return, he flashed her a brilliant smile that he'd probably been using since the cradle to unhinge women of all ages. In any case, it completely undid the poor waitress for a minute before she snapped out of it and remembered what she did for a living. "Oh," she said as she lifted up the bottle of wine she'd been holding and showed it to Alec. "I almost forgot. Compliments of the Baldwins."

While Daisy turned toward the Baldwins and acknowledged the gift with a smile and a little wave, the waitress opened the bottle. After Alec sampled it, he nodded his approval.

"I was going to say we should thank them on our way out," he said as the waitress filled their glasses. "But it appears we'll be saved the trip."

Daisy turned her head to follow his gaze and saw the Baldwins headed their way.

"Hello, you two," Virginia said in a sing-song voice as they approached. She leaned down and gave Daisy a kiss on the cheek. "You look stunning."

"That's what I told her," Alec said. "But she didn't believe me."

Joseph laughed. "Tell her again. Women need to hear the good stuff a couple of times before it sinks in."

Alec looked over at her, his smile soft, his eyes deep pools of blue. "I'll give that a try, sir."

Oh, Lord, she thought as she melted into that gentle smile that threatened to melt her hard-won protective core. *Mustn't be alone with him. Not for a moment.* "Would you two like to join us?" Daisy asked, pasting on a smile she didn't feel. "We'd love it, wouldn't we, Alec?" she asked and dared him with narrowed eyes to dispute her claim.

Alec considered the question. He wanted to say, "Actually, no. That would completely ruin my evening. And with you suddenly looking like you just stepped off a runway, I find it particularly inconvenient, thank you." But, instead, he mechanically repeated her, "We'd love it."

"That's so sweet of you," Virginia said as she reached out and patted his hand in that grandmotherly way he'd only ever seen in the movies. "But we're just on our way out. Enjoy your dinner, you two."

And with that, Alec's favorite clients departed and he found himself blissfully alone with his very flustered and very beautiful former assistant.

Everything about her was changed, from her hair—tossed into a wild, messy style that made him think about what it would be like to wake up next to her after a long, steamy night—right down to the clingy, designer clothes of which he most thoroughly approved. The truth of it was, he thought as he settled back into his chair and continued to admire her, sometime in the last six hours, Daisy Kincaid had morphed into a temptation he wasn't sure he could deny himself.

"What?" she asked, tugging at her dark hair.

"Nothing," he said and was very happy she couldn't read his thoughts.

"You're staring."

Get used to it. "Sorry," he said and picked up a menu. "Ready to order?"

Exasperation rang in her voice when she said, "You're really not leaving?"

He smiled at her, looking even more beautiful now that she was annoyed. "I wouldn't dream of letting you eat alone."

"Dream away," she said, nodding encouragingly. "I don't mind."

Oh, no. No way was he walking away from her tonight. "Nothing doing. You're in for the pleasure of my company for the rest of the evening."

After a moment, she picked up her own menu. "Lucky me," she muttered as she began to study it intensely.

He watched as concentration made her subtly lipsticked mouth pucker into a perfect bow. If he didn't kiss her by the end of the night it would be an act of will, he thought as he dragged his fingers through his hair and wondered why he suddenly felt like his life was slipping beyond his control.

Was it because the Baldwins had held his feet to the fire to bring Daisy back onto the project? Or was it because Daisy had recently revealed several troubling aspects of what he presumed was her true nature—stubborn and sexy foremost among them? Or maybe it was because now he had to deal with this…this metamorphosis that was making it impossible to think of anything but taking her back to their hotel room and making love to her until he got her out of his system.

And he would, he knew. He always did. All he could give any woman was a week, maybe two, and then he started to feel smothered and he stopped calling and it was uncomfortable for a while and then it was over. That's how it normally went.

But this didn't feel normal—and not just because he couldn't pull his standard disappearing act on someone who worked for him and who shared his hotel room. No, this didn't feel normal because Daisy was different from other women. He *liked* Daisy. He liked being with her, liked talking to her. Hell, right now he was enjoying just looking at her.

The waitress returned and they ordered their food before surrendering their menus and the wine list. Then, with nothing to hide behind, Daisy looked up at him with an expression that plainly said, "Now what?" Her fine eyebrows were arched over brown eyes outlined in a dark, smoky color that made them look positively luminous; her skin was flawless in the candlelight; her full lips were tipped up slightly at the corners.

Now what, indeed, he thought, because at that moment, all he could think about was how much he wanted this woman in his arms, in his bed…

"So," he said as he shifted in his chair to take the pressure off the places that needed to depressurize, "tell me what you're going to do when this job is over."

She sat back and regarded him quizzically, as if it was the last thing she'd expected him to say. "I don't know. Find another job?"

"You could always stay," he said, then wished he could

take those words back because right now, he wasn't so sure
having a temptation like her hanging around the office was
such a hot idea.

But he needn't have worried because she was already
shaking her head. "Not a chance. Besides, I have a plan."

"Another plan?" The blush that stained her cheeks let him
know that she'd caught his reference. The last time she'd had
"a plan," they'd ended up making out on a public sidewalk. He
felt a tide of heat rush through him at the memory.

"Not like that. A real plan. A career." She shook her head.
"Anyway, it doesn't matter…" And then her words trailed off,
the conversational equivalent of closing a door.

"Tell me," he said and the intensity in his voice surprised
him. Check out Mr. Self-Involved, he thought. Caring about
the future of this troubling woman.

"I don't think so," she said, staring down into her wineglass.
"I mean, I've never told anyone before. Not even my brothers."

"Look, after your tour of duty is done here, you'll probably never see me again," he said. *Maybe.* "So who's a better
choice than me?"

She took a deep swallow of wine, then looked into his
eyes, wordlessly daring him to mock her. "You'll think it's
silly," she said. "But it's always been a dream of mine to own
a bed-and-breakfast."

It would be perfect, of course. She'd been organizing,
hosting, entertaining and charming Mackenzie clients for
years. But why hadn't she told him about it before? After all,
if he'd known, he could have done something. Hell, he would
have…what? What would he have done? Probably, he
thought as equal measures of guilt and regret pressed down
on him, he wouldn't have done anything at all.

Alec sat back in his chair and marveled that so much had changed between them in such a short time. "You'd be excellent at that," he said as he smiled into her wary gaze. "Do you need an architect?"

She smiled back, tentatively at first. "I will, I suppose. Someday. But that's like, step 175. I'm still at step one."

"What step was graduating from college?"

"Okay," she said, her smile growing wider. "Then I'm at step two."

He leaned forward. "And negotiating that sweet deal to be the comanager of a job that involves rebuilding a couple of swank B & B's right here in Santa Margarita?" Strange how that fact failed to give him the same twinge of anger it had just a day or two ago. What was up with that?

She chuckled. "Touché," she said and made a check mark in the air. "Step three."

"All right then. What's next?" he asked, and watched, mesmerized, as her smile ratcheted up to full wattage.

Eyes sparkling, she asked, "Do you really want to know?"

"Absolutely," he said, and refilled her wineglass.

Dinner passed quickly. Daisy, more animated than he'd ever seen her, told him about her dreams, shared her ideas and described some truly innovative concepts for the bed-and-breakfast she'd been planning, it turned out, ever since she was a young girl. Her level of enthusiasm was so infectious, he could feel himself smiling foolishly at her while she spoke.

By the time they walked out of the restaurant, Alec felt as though he knew Daisy better than he knew just about anyone. Under normal circumstances that fact alone would've scared him out of his mind. Instead it just felt right.

The cool, damp sea air swirled around them, making

Daisy's skirt flutter distractingly about her legs. "Walk me home?" she asked.

And even though his golf cart was parked just around the corner, he took the heavy shopping bags from her hands and said, "Lead the way, innkeeper," and loved the feeling of her laughter shimmering through him.

Their path was lit by the mellow beams of the street-lamps as they walked side by side toward their hotel. Music poured into the harbor from bars and restaurants, revelers spilled out onto patios, teenagers laughed loudly as they fooled around on the narrow stretch of beach. But for Alec, the only things that mattered were the way Daisy's shoulder kept brushing up against his and the scent of her on the whispering breeze and the almost overwhelming urge he had to take her in his arms and kiss her until she was breathless.

Alec tried to shake the image out of his head as their hotel came into view. He'd always been very careful not to let a woman wield any sort of power over him and he wasn't about to start now—especially when he was about to be tested by spending another night under the same roof with her.

When they got to their room, Daisy unlocked the door and stepped inside ahead of Alec. He was closing it behind him when he heard her exclaim, "Oh, Alec," in a high, excited voice. "They're absolutely gorgeous. Where did you—"

"What are you talking about?" he asked as he came up behind her.

"These," she said as she moved out of the way to reveal the huge bouquet of red roses that had been placed on the main worktable in their absence.

Alarm bells clanged inside his head as she reached for the

card stuck in between the blooms. Were they from Tom the Hunk? he wondered as she tore open the card in that impatient way women have when flowers are at issue.

Daisy bit into her bottom lip as she read the note. Then she glanced very, very briefly at Alec.

"Well?" he asked, his good humor dimming in the face of the mystery.

She slipped the note back into the tiny envelope. "Well what?"

"Who are they from?" he asked and instantly wished his voice hadn't sounded so edgy. Jeez, he was really starting to lose it.

"They're from Troy," she said, her chin tipping up defiantly.

Troy? Where did that guy get off sending flowers to Daisy? he thought as he stepped closer. He wasn't nearly good enough for her. But then again, what guy was? "What does he want?" Alec growled.

"He doesn't *want* anything," she said as she spun around quickly and bumped right into Alec's chest. She took a deep breath and stared at the white buttons on his shirt for a moment. "That is," she finally said to the shirt, "we made a date for tomorrow morning and he sent these to remind me."

"A date?" he said, only just realizing that he'd been half hoping both he and Daisy would be too tired from a night of lovemaking to do much of anything tomorrow morning. "To do what?" he asked.

"You're being nosy again." She held up a hand when he opened his mouth to speak. "Or overprotective. Either way, I don't want to hear it."

"As your friend, I have to say—"

"Don't," she warned.

"But—"

She covered her ears with her palms. "I'm not listening."

"Fine," he said, then reached out to take her hands away from her ears. "Fine," he repeated as he pulled her hands to his chest and held them tight. "But just in case he turns out to be a serial killer, tell me where you're going so I can let the police know where they should start looking for your mangled body."

She frowned at their entwined hands but didn't pull away. Then she looked up at him and said with a sort of wonder, "You're unbelievable."

Damn. The closer he got, the prettier she was. The freckles that dusted her nose stood out on her silken skin and her beautiful brown eyes danced with gold flecks. Her bottom lip was caught between her straight, white teeth and... Lord, how was he ever going to forget what those lips felt like beneath his own?

"So are you," he whispered, and reached out to sweep back a curl that had fallen over her forehead.

Daisy's lips parted, but he didn't wait to hear what she had to say. Words weren't getting them anywhere, anyway. So in one fluid movement, he tugged her closer, lowered his head and did exactly what he'd been thinking about all damn day.

Alec Mackenzie was kissing her, Daisy thought even as her knees went wobbly and her lips went pliant. Alec Mackenzie was kissing *her*. And before she had time to wrap her mind around that fact, his mouth suddenly slanted against hers, the pressure maddeningly light, polite almost to the point of pain. She tugged ineffectually to get her hands free from where they were pinned between their bodies so she could pull him closer but he stilled her with a barely uttered, "Shhh," and then picked right back up where he left off.

Holy smokes. This was mistake, she thought, a colossal mistake. And then she moaned into his mouth as his tongue swept teasingly inside and met hers, sending shivers of pure need through her.

One more minute. She'd enjoy this exquisite feeling for one more minute and then she'd be able to pull away without regrets, without wishing she could stay in his arms all night tonight. And tomorrow night. And then maybe a few more.

Damn.

"Golf," she said against his lips.

He stilled, as she knew he would. Then he tipped his forehead against hers and whispered, "Golf?"

"I'm playing golf in the morning," she said, forcing herself to step back and take her hands and her heart with her. "An early tee time, too, so I really should hit the sack."

"I see," he said, but she could tell just by the tone of his voice that he really didn't see at all.

But it didn't matter. She had no idea what he was up to this time, but she wasn't going to fall for it. Nope, she thought as she bade Alec a hasty good-night, picked up her shopping bags and fled to her room like the chicken-hearted coward she was. The only thing that could come from heading down the path they'd just been on was more heartbreak for her.

And she had pretty much done her time in the Heartbreak Hotel for this lifetime. At least, she thought as she closed her bedroom door without daring to look back, she hoped she had.

Seven

Daisy teed up a ball at the Santa Margarita Golf Club's driving range, set up in front of it, wiggled her spikes into the Astroturf and adjusted her grip. Then she did what she'd done millions of times since she'd picked up her first nine iron when she was eight years old: she swung her club in a perfect arc, smacked that little white ball dead on, heard the satisfying ping that signaled she'd hit the club's sweet spot and watched the ball fly past one yard marker after another until it finally settled just behind the sign that read two hundred yards.

Not bad for a set of loaner clubs, she thought as she let the three wood slide out of her hand and into the bright red bag she'd picked up at the pro shop a half hour earlier. And thank goodness she'd needed to borrow these clubs, too, because that's how the golf pro had found her in time to give her a message from Troy. He wasn't going to be able to meet her like they'd planned, the pro had told her, because he'd gotten a last-minute charter and wouldn't be back until late afternoon. Before he'd left, the pro had assured her that the tee time was still hers, and since she really needed to blow off some steam leftover from last night, she'd decided to go ahead and play alone.

Daisy smiled grimly as she hefted the bag onto her shoulder and headed back to the pro shop to pick up her golf cart. In a way, it was a relief that Troy hadn't been able to make it. When she'd accepted the date the other night, she'd thought it would be a positive step in her efforts to move on with her life. But after being in Alec's arms again last night, she knew that even if she dated every eligible man in North America, it wasn't going to help her get over him.

The answer was probably time, unfortunately. And some distance would be helpful, too, but it didn't look as if she was going to get much of that in the near future. The best she could hope for now, she thought as she dropped her bag in the rack outside the pro shop, was to finish this job with her sanity intact.

"You need a caddy today, ma'am?"

Daisy turned around, ready to smile and decline—after all, she'd been carrying a full bag since the fifth grade—but could only stare in mute shock when she saw that Alec had been the one making the offer.

"Hey, Daze," he said, and his voice was like warm honey pouring over her cold soul.

"What are you doing here, Alec?" she asked, even as her stomach did an unexpected little flip-flop at the sight of him.

"I've been thinking," he said as he reached around her and

opened the door to the pro shop. "I really haven't been holding up my end of that bargain we made when you agreed to come back to work." At her baffled look, he added, "You know, the errand boy thing. So I thought a perfect way to make good would be to caddy for you today."

For one long second Daisy was speechless. They *had* made that deal as they'd stood haggling in her kitchen, but why did he have to offer to pay up now, she thought, when she was trying her damnedest to get over him?

She stomped into the shop and walked up to the counter. "I don't need a caddy, Alec. In fact, I'm just picking up the key for a golf cart, so as you can see—"

"Where's the flyboy?" Alec asked, looking around the shop as if Troy might be hiding behind a rack of plaid pants.

"Well," she said, stalling. "He, uh, couldn't make it. An important business thing, I guess." And then, because her face was burning, she turned her back on him and waited for the clerk to bring her the key.

"So what you really need, then," he said as pinned her against the counter by standing behind her and bracing his hands on either side of her body, "is a new golf partner."

What I need, she thought as the heat of his body seared into her, is to get a grip on myself. A potent blend of excitement, anger and anticipation rose up inside her, higher and higher, making it all but impossible to come up with a witty response. In the end, the best she could do was to breathe in and out, in and out, while she tried to analyze the situation at hand.

Was this the same man who, just a few days ago, had acted as if he didn't care that she'd quit and then had come to her with his hat in his hands? Was this the same man who'd pushed her away when she'd kissed him—heat rose higher in her cheeks as she relived that particular episode in her mind—and then last night had kissed *her*? It was the same man, of course, and now, here he was, standing way inside her personal space, trying to melt her down to her bone marrow with nothing more than the pressure of his body against her back.

Alec leaned down and whispered into her ear, "What do you say?"

"No, thanks," she squeaked as she signaled to the clerk. "I don't mind spending a little time alone. Golf is like meditation to me."

"In that case, I'll be as quiet as a monk at prayer."

"No, really," she began, ready to make up something about the Zen of golf, but he interrupted her first.

"Of course," he said as he plucked the golf cart key out of the clerk's hand, "that game you and I played at Riviera was pretty close. You're probably afraid I'll beat you."

She spun away from him and backed up a step or two. "That wouldn't happen, Alec. I don't want to be mean, but I'm just better than you."

There was no indication that she'd riled him, but there was a healthy dose of something incredibly wicked in his eyes that made her feel like fanning herself to cool off.

"You want to make a little bet?" he asked.

Even though he'd been playing dirty ever since he'd taken her in his arms last night, she wanted to be fair. "Alec, I'll beat you."

"If you're so sure, Buddha, make a bet for something you really want."

A really brazen woman would take the bet. A brazen

woman would bet a night of passion or—hey, he was loaded—a week on a private island with him as her personal boy toy.

Daisy, however, wasn't brazen. She was a chicken.

"What do you want to bet?" she asked, even as she realized she'd just implied that he could join her for this round of golf.

He leaned against the counter and appeared to consider it. "How about this," he said after a moment. "I win, you keep working for Mackenzie when this job is done. You win, I invest in your dream."

He'd never win, so she didn't give the idea of working for him in the future a second thought. She, however, *was* going to win, so she pushed her luck. "How big an investment?"

"A hundred percent."

"I can't let you do that," she said, shocked that he would even consider it.

"I won't have to," he said smugly. "I'm going to win."

Why, the arrogant little rat. She put out a hand to shake on their new deal and said, "Fine." But when he took her hand in his, instead of shaking it, he lifted it to his lips and brushed a kiss across her heated skin. Oh, Lord, she thought as she pulled her hand away. She wasn't fine. For starters, her body was on fire, her heart was beating too fast and her mind was a mess.

Daisy watched Alec test the grips on a set of loaner clubs while he whistled like a crazy, tone-deaf parakeet. If she was going to win—and she *was* going to win—she had to calm down. But since she didn't really know anything about Zen or meditation or even Buddha, she decided she'd simply try to ignore him.

To that end, she left the shop while he was still paying for his clubs, picked up her bag where she'd left it and walked to the cart. But even as she was trying to figure out how to turn "ignore him" into a mantra, she felt him walking up behind her, a demon in crisp khakis.

She made an effort to focus on something other than how wonderfully encouraging he'd been about her plans to open a B & B—and how she'd felt when he'd kissed her last night—to get him out of her mind. The clank of the clubs as they banged against each other in the bag, the billowing clouds rolling lazily in from the sea, the scratching of a gardener's rake somewhere off to their left.

"Mind if I drive?" Alec asked as he lifted the bag off her shoulder and secured it in the cart.

"Are you going to drive it like it's your Ferrari?"

There was a sinister glint in his eye when he asked, "Scared?"

"Terrified," she said, and she kind of meant it.

"Good." He got into the cart and fired up the sputtering electric engine. Then he stepped on the pedal hard and the cart lurched forward which made Daisy grab for the dash in a panic.

"You can hang on to me if you need to," he said with a chuckle.

"No, thank you," she said, digging her short nails into her palms and trying not to fall out onto the grass in an unladylike heap.

When they got to the first hole, he jumped out and pulled her clubs off the cart. "The fairway doglegs to the left on this hole at about two hundred yards so you might—"

She rolled her eyes and beckoned with her gloved right hand for him to give her the bag. "Just give it to me," she said.

"Careful what you ask for, little girl," he said in that damned honeyed voice.

Hot to the roots of her hair, she shot him what she hoped was a stern look and reached out to grab her clubs from him. Unfortunately her timing was off, and their fingers got tangled up on the shoulder strap and that caused heat from his touch to trickle through her and spread down her body like butter melting over a stack of pancakes. It wasn't graceful, but in about half a second she managed to wrest the bag from him, yank it on to her shoulder and scamper away to safety.

By the time she'd made it to the lady's tee box, she was ready to concede defeat just to get away from him. The thing was, though, if she did that she'd lose the bet and then she'd have to keep working for him for God knew how long.

That was all it took to get her mind back in the game. If nothing else, her brothers had taught her how to go to war on the golf course. And this guy needed to be brought down a notch or two in a very big way.

"What do you think," Alec called out to her, "a three wood?"

She looked up at him where he stood at the men's tee a few yards away. "What happened to the monk at prayer routine you promised?"

"Went out the window with the bet," he said with a grin.

She took a tee from the pocket of her shorts and bent over to anchor it into the grass, then set a ball atop it. "Watch and learn," she said, plucking a two iron from the bag. "Watch and learn."

"Oh, I plan to," he said and something in his voice made her glance up. His smile had dimmed and something about his posture made him look a little tense but other than that, he looked okay.

Really okay. Great, in fact. Gorgeous.

"Do you have a problem?" she asked in complete exasperation.

"No. Absolutely not. Best day of my life." He set his own bag down and pulled his glove out of his pocket. "Fire away."

She adjusted her grip and cursed the uncharacteristic tremble in her hands. Then she gritted her teeth, summoned the gods of golf to help her play well—in spite of the hunky, six-foot-tall distraction standing just outside her line of sight—and prepared to take her first swing in what she already knew was going to be the longest eighteen holes of her life.

Alec couldn't take his eyes off her as she waggled and wiggled and took aim at the little dimpled ball that lay between her feet. Above her trim ankles, her toned, tanned legs looked like a long, lovely stretch of paradise below the exquisite curve of her perfect, tempting, round…

Ping!

The sound shook him from his daydream, and he shaded his eyes as he watched her ball fly straight and true until it fell decisively into the center of the fairway nearly two hundred yards away.

"That's your fault," she said as she spun around and pointed the club at him like it was a sword aimed at his heart.

"What are you talking about? That was a great shot."

"Could have been better if someone wasn't purposely trying to distract me."

He put a hand to his chest. "Me? I'm like the soul of peace and tranquility over here."

She looked heavenward and the thought came to him without warning: I love getting under her skin. This was naturally followed by a more lascivious thought about her and her skin, one that he shouldn't be thinking if he wanted to win this game—which he most definitely did—so he turned away from her and got ready to take his own shot.

He'd been flirting with her, he thought to himself as he looked down the fairway, and that was not a great idea. In fact, it was an idea that would undoubtedly lead to more sleepless nights just like last night and the night before. But dammit, he was truly enjoying himself—which, now that he thought about it, he didn't do nearly often enough—so he was just going to play this game, win their bet, keep her on the pay-roll and see what happened.

Anyway, it wasn't as if he hadn't tried to put her out of his mind last night. It's just that she wouldn't go. Her scent clung to his sweater, his lips burned where they'd touched hers, her smile and laugh and contagious optimism staked out places in his mind and refused to budge.

So that's why, after making a few quick phone calls this morning to make sure Troy would be way too busy to play golf, here he was, thoroughly enjoying himself and well on his way to winning a bet that would land Daisy right back where she belonged: with him, five days a week, just like it used to be.

No matter how attracted he was to her, he still wasn't willing to sacrifice their...whatever this was for a week or two in the hay. But after a second night of tossing and turning, he also knew he wasn't willing to let her out of his life completely.

"We playing golf today, Mackenzie?" the lady in question called out.

He smiled to himself as he addressed the ball, then pulled the club back and executed a pretty damn good swing. He kept his club high as he watched the ball soar, then frowned when it hooked slightly and landed far to the left but slightly closer to the pin than Daisy's.

Okay, stop thinking about her and play, you idiot. She was good—possibly better than him, even—but oh-so-easily flustered. And he planned to exploit that fact to the limits of good sportsmanship.

Alec whistled a few random, off-key notes as he replaced his club, shouldered his bag and met up with Daisy at the cart. When he slid behind the wheel, she was smiling ear to ear.

"Counting chickens before they're hatched, are we?" he asked.

"I'm just daydreaming about the B & B I'm going to own soon," she said as she sat back and crossed her arms, pushing her breasts up high enough to make him forget what he'd been thinking about a moment earlier.

"Don't sign the lease yet, sweetheart," he said as he tore his gaze away from that distracting sight. "We have seventeen and a half holes to go." And with that, he pushed the pedal to the floor again just to bug her.

Someday, when he had enough perspective to look back on this and laugh, Alec would probably remember that he didn't really start to sweat until they hit the turn after the ninth hole.

They were at the snack bar, grabbing a little fuel before they started the next nine holes and Daisy was just walking back to their table with some fruit and a bottle of water. Her hips swayed unselfconsciously, her smile was sweet, satisfaction shone in her eyes.

That's when he realized he was in trouble. And not just because she was kicking his butt—although she was, quite handily. She was six over par—a very respectable score, no matter how you sliced it. He, however, was fifteen over par. *Fifteen.* Unless he started channeling Tiger Woods very soon, she'd have to lose a limb to get far enough behind to even this match up.

But he was in bigger trouble than just losing this game, he thought as he watched her take a bite of her apple, then lick a little of its juice off her bottom lip. Good Lord. Such a simple gesture and yet it made him want to throw her over his shoulder like a caveman and take her back to the hotel and lock her up. With him. For about a week.

She smiled at him as she nibbled the apple. "Penny for your thoughts."

"Not a chance," he said as he stood and looked up at the sky. "Those clouds don't look good. Let's get going."

So they started again, but after Daisy put her ball on the eleventh green in one shot, she looked over at him with her cheeks flushed from the wind, her eyes bright with pleasure, her hair doing that damned I-just-woke-up-after-a-night-of-incredible-sex thing and an unexpected and painful twinge contracted right in the center of Alec's chest. Something, he thought as he stared at her, was desperately wrong. And that something was that he actually wanted this woman enough to break his rules.

He pulled out his pitching wedge and stomped off into the boonies to look for his own ball, the one that had strayed into the thick rough with his last shot. And all the while he was thinking, "This is not going to happen." Because even though he wanted Daisy, it wasn't in the way that Daisy wanted to be wanted, the way she deserved to be wanted. At least, he was pretty sure that was true.

The steely-gray clouds that had been gathering overhead

had cooled the temperature considerably since they'd begun the round, but that didn't keep Alec from burning deep inside. Knowing that he wanted her enough to bend, break and annihilate his permanent rules didn't make any difference because he still didn't have anything to offer her. All he had was a bad track record, a short attention span and a big, bad, unshakable desire to see her naked.

Soon.

Alec was mumbling to himself and checking behind a large, ornery-looking yucca plant a few yards off the course when Daisy called out, "Need some help in there? I can try to find an Indian scout to help out if you want."

He growled an impolite response he hoped she couldn't hear, but when she appeared by his side a moment later, he could tell that she had. "Sorry," he said. "Uncalled for."

She waved a hand. "Three brothers, remember? I've heard it all." Then she moved away from him and started to look through the heavy foliage for his ball. "You're in pretty deep, huh?"

Am I ever. "Nothing I can't work out," he said, searching halfheartedly while he watched her walk around a eucalyptus. His heart twinged again, and the furious beating of it hammered at him relentlessly.

Alec looked up at the sky and the clouds whose intentions were now painted in ominous shades of gray. And even though he didn't believe in much, he believed enough to ask whoever was up there what he'd done to deserve this mess. Then, like a memo from God, a raindrop hit him square in the eye.

Well, that's an answer, he thought as he looked back down—and saw his ball tucked beneath a big, healthy sage.

The rain picked up and began falling in sharp, wet *splats* as he walked over and tried to figure out how in the hell he was going to get his ball back onto the green with one swing. When he finally straightened and prepared to take aim, Daisy called out, "What are you doing?"

"Hopefully," he said without looking up, "getting this in the hole with one more shot."

"It's raining," she said.

"Yep." Then he pulled back and took a short, chopping swing. The ball lifted, took flight and landed gloriously on the edge of the green.

The rain was really starting to come down when he went to his bag and switched his wedge for a putter. His ball was farther from the cup than hers, so he took his putt and, a moment later, the ball sank into the hole with a satisfying clatter.

"Happy?" she hollered over the relentless *splat, splat* of the rain.

Alec looked over his shoulder and saw her sitting in the driver's seat of the cart. "What are you doing?" he asked.

"I'm going home." When he didn't say anything, she added, "Alec, it's *raining*."

"But we're not finished." He wiped rivulets of water off his face. "We have a bet to settle."

Daisy smiled and pointed up at the sky. "Let's just call it a draw on account of an Act of God, okay?"

A draw? Alec had never played to a draw. He won or he lost—although, to be honest, he usually won. Anyway, they had to finish this. They'd bet their futures on it. "You can't do that."

"Sure I can."

"But you're winning," he said as he slung his bag over his shoulder and walked toward the cart. Water splashed up with each step he took.

She shrugged. "I don't care if I win."

"Of course you do."

She looked at him as if he'd lost his mind. "No, I really don't. *I don't care if I win.*"

"But, Daisy," he said without bothering to keep the impatience out of his voice. "Winning is what matters."

"No, Alec," she said with a look that he was quite sure bordered on pity. "Being happy, having fun, enjoying your life and the people in it. That's what matters."

In a flash so brief it felt like a part of a dream long forgotten, he saw life the way it could be—love and happiness, fulfillment and peace, family and joy. Then it disappeared and the twinge in his heart squeezed harder. And even though he knew he would never be able to put into words what had happened today, he knew with complete certainty that his life was never going to be the same.

When he'd made the bet, he'd been so sure he'd win, he'd told himself he'd invest in her business even when she came back to work for him. With her working for him and starting a new business, there'd have been some logistics to work out, of course, but he'd been willing. If they declared it a draw, he was sure he'd never see her again after they were done with this project.

He put his clubs in the cart and she smiled a little. "Let's go home and get warm," she said as she rubbed her arms.

"You go on without me," he said, feeling strangely hollow. "My cart's in the parking lot." He jerked his thumb over his shoulder as he watched the rain sweep, tsunami-style, across

the smooth grass behind her. "I'll just meet you back at the…"
He hesitated, then said, "Back at home."

She laughed, obviously thinking he was kidding, but she
stopped when he said, "No, really. I need the walk."

She stared at him through the rain, and the expression on
her pretty face betrayed everything: curiosity, concern and
that certain something that was Daisy's alone—an appealing,
unwavering niceness that marked her as the perfect girl next
door. "You're serious," she said finally.

"Very." *Now go before I change my mind and jump in that
cart and take you away somewhere where I can keep you all
to myself for as long as you'll let me.* "See you at home," he
said and hit the roof a couple of times with an open palm.

The cool rain needled into Alec's arms and face as he
watched Daisy drive slowly away, then he turned up the
wholly inadequate collar of his golf shirt and took off toward
the clubhouse.

Home. Daisy had said it first, before he'd sent her away.
Let's go home. The word haunted him, made him feel like a
man stranded in a world where he'd never belonged. Only a
word, but it was so intimate it made him shiver.

He slogged down the path, and his wet sneakers made a
schlock-schlock sound with each step he took. And all the
while, like a splinter digging into his mind, Alec wondered
just one thing—what would it be like to share a home with
Daisy. Share a home. He, who couldn't even commit to a
houseplant, for chrissakes.

When you're walking in a freak thunderstorm on the wide-
open landscape of a golf course, the minutes pass like hours.
That's probably why it seemed like he'd been walking forever when a low hum sounded behind him and began to grow

louder. Perhaps it's a swarm of killer bees, he thought grimly. But when he realized the sound was only the buzzing motor of an approaching golf cart, he shoved his hands in his pockets, put his head down against the rain and kept on walking.

Eight

Before Daisy had made it halfway back to the clubhouse, it was clear that the storm was going to get a whole lot worse before it got better.

The rain slanted into the cart as she drove down the golf path and peered through the rain-streaked windshield at the darkening gloom ahead. Her sweater was soaked through to her skin, but she knew it was nothing compared to the drenching Alec must be getting right now.

Something twisted inside Daisy when she remembered how he'd looked in the rearview mirror as she'd driven away from him. His dark hair plastered to his head; his white golf shirt sopping wet and clinging to his hard, muscled chest and arms; his frown deep and growing deeper.

She should have insisted that he come with her, she thought. She should have been the cooler head. But when it had started to rain and he'd been so adamant about continuing their game, she'd simply lost patience with his *über*-competitive, win-at-all-costs attitude. It was a guy thing, she knew, but still, a nice walk in the cool rain ought to make him think twice before he made crazy, unwinnable bets and then refused to stop playing in a monsoon, for crying out loud.

Alec was, bar none, the most competitive person she'd ever met. Now that she thought about it, it was probably that same spirit that made him such a playboy. Hit-and-run conquests, one after another after another. He had no lasting relationships that she knew of—if you didn't count his best friend, Todd—and he seemed to like it that way.

Thank God she hadn't lost the bet. Working with him day in and day out had always been hard, but working with him permanently would have been even harder now that she knew him better…and impossible now that she knew that she was in love with him.

She was in love with Alec Mackenzie. There, she'd said it. Of course, she'd probably been in love all along and just hadn't been able to admit it, but spending so much time with him *sans* bimbos had changed, intensified and complicated everything.

Love, she thought with a sigh. She had to be the unluckiest girl in the world.

She slowed the cart and made a clumsy U-turn. Even though she knew Alec would never return the sentiment, it would be bad form if she stood by while he caught pneumonia and died, so she completed her turn and headed back to find him.

It didn't take her long. He was the only stubborn, wet, muddy man for miles around.

When she came up alongside him and he turned to look

at her, she had to stifle a laugh. Water dripped from his storm-mussed hair, and one trembling drop hung precariously from the tip of his nose. His clothes were drenched and painted with fresh streaks of mud. His eyes were like blue fire and his mouth tipped down gravely at the corners. He looked like a big, fierce dog who'd been left out in the rain by mistake.

"Ready to swallow your pride?"

"You know me better than that," he said and kept on walking. Water spattered beneath his feet with each step.

"Alec, I'm not leaving you out here in the rain. I'll just drive alongside you until we get to the parking lot. We'll look ridiculous. You might as well get in."

He glanced at her and she watched as a raindrop fell from the long lashes that had, in her opinion, been unfairly given to a man. He squeegeed the rain off his face with a swipe of his hand and said, "Thanks, but we're almost there."

Frustration, hot and fluid, flowed over her and sent her good sense packing. "You know what's wrong with you, Alec?" she said, and was surprised at the rough, bitter edge in her own voice.

"No," he said on a sigh. "But I'm pretty sure you're going to tell me."

"You keep everyone at arm's length."

He shrugged again but kept on walking. "So what?"

"So what?" Daisy asked in exasperation. "So you move from one superficial relationship to the next as fast as you can. Your Rolodex is full of people you don't really know. You spend every Christmas in Hawaii with the flavor of the month." She tried to stop the gush of words but it was like a dam had burst. "For God's sake, Alec, you call your mother by her first name! Don't you care about anyone? Were you raised by wolves or something?"

He laughed harshly. "I wish," he joked, but there was something about his manner that made her wonder how close to the bone she'd just cut.

But she never had a chance to find out because in the next moment, he came around to the driver's side, grabbed the steering wheel and swung his big body inside the cart while it was still moving. She had no choice but to scoot away from his wet but disconcertingly warm body and the press of his leg against hers and let him drive.

"Actually," he said casually, as if she hadn't just been hijacked, "I can prove that I do care about someone."

"What are you talking about?" she asked as she slumped down in the seat and folded her arms to ward off the cold.

"While it may be true that I keep most people at arm's length," he said, draping his arm over the back of the bench seat. "I cared enough about you to make sure you didn't get hurt today."

Daisy went hot and cold in sharp, uncomfortable waves. He cared about her, he'd said. But what was that about her getting hurt? "Get hurt by what?" she asked, even as she noticed that he was driving right past the pro shop without returning their clubs or the golf cart.

"Troy, of course."

What did Troy have to do with this? "What are you talking about? And where are you going?" she asked as they whizzed through the parking lot and turned onto the road that led to back down to town.

"Troy's a loser, Daze," Alec said. "He only wants one

thing from you. So I made sure he was too busy to keep his date with you today."

Oh, my God. He couldn't have *paid* Troy to bail out on their date. Even he wouldn't be that asinine, would he? But she forced herself to unclench her jaw and ask, just for the record. "What did you do, Alec?"

"I just arranged for him to have a very lucrative job offered to him this morning."

It took an awful lot to get Daisy mad—her brothers were experts at it—but Alec had just managed to raise her dormant temper in nothing flat. She counted to ten and struggled to take a big, deep cleansing breath like the eerily serene instructor on her yoga tape had taught her.

"He's not good enough for you," Alec said before she could finish her breathing.

Of course. He'd already told her he felt responsible for her but hearing it again made her just as mad as it had the first time. If only he'd been able to see her as a woman instead of someone to watch over, maybe they could have...

Stick to the subject at hand, she told herself as he slowed to a stop at a signal. "Like I told you before," she said calmly. "I have three brothers. I don't need another one."

He gave her a smoky look that would've curled her toes if they weren't so cold. His blue bedroom eyes were at half-mast, one side of his sensual mouth was lifted up in a sexy smile, his wet hair dipped over his forehead carelessly. Then he leaned over and whispered into her ear, his voice whiskey deep, "Believe me when I tell you that being *brotherly* was the last thing on my mind."

Then her toes really did curl.

Don't go there, her slim grasp on sanity warned as he

turned onto their street and the wind blew a fresh sheet of rain violently into the windshield. Whatever his reasons for following her today really were, they were not to be interpreted as anything more than him sticking his nose where it didn't belong out of some misguided sense of duty. What was happening here was that Alec was drenched, dirty and spoiling for a fight. And she was just the girl to give it to him.

"Alec," she said, "you're the one that spreads yourself as thin as melted butter, using women and throwing them away like dirty Kleenex as fast as you can. That's not Troy. That's *you*."

A cloud passed over his expression briefly as he steered the cart into the Hotel Margarita's parking lot. Then he gave her a look that had "And your point is?" written all over it, which ratcheted up her ire about a dozen notches.

"Given that you seem to think a satisfying ending to a relationship is to dodge phone calls until they give up," she continued with undisguised impatience, "you may find this impossible to understand. But I'm an optimist so I'm going to say it anyway. Troy is my friend. A friend, who, I can assure you, is not interested in me in the way you think."

His laughter came out in a short bark. "Women always say that. You haven't got a clue who's interested in you."

But I sure know who's not interested, she thought as he cut the engine just outside their room and her anger reached boiling temperature.

"Trust me," he said, "when I tell you that Troy is interested in you. You just don't see it." Then he jumped out of the cart and ran through the rain to the relative safety of their front door.

Infuriated, she followed. When they reached the shelter of

the bougainvillea-covered trellis that arched over their entry-
way, she said, "I think I'd know, Alec."

"No, you wouldn't.

"Yes, I would."

"Wouldn't."

With a vicious stab, she stuck her key in the door's lock.
"Would."

She was so engrossed in the argument that she almost
jumped out of her skin when Alec, in lieu of a comeback,
clamped his hands down on her shoulders and turned her toward him roughly. In the glow of the porch light, his gaze was
fiery, evangelical.

"You know why I'm sure you wouldn't see it if someone
was attracted to you, Daisy?" He paused, his fingers tighten-
ing on her shoulders. "Because you don't even know that I'm
about to kiss you."

The last thing Daisy remembered thinking before thinking became way too much trouble was, "He's absolutely
right."

She never saw it coming, never would have guessed it
would happen, and yet Alec was pulling her close and his demanding lips were capturing hers in a hungry kiss that swept
away any rational thought with the first, hot thrust of his
tongue.

His haste thrilled her, filled her with resolve. This is
what she'd waited for, what she'd longed for, what she'd
imagined a thousand times when she closed her eyes. And
while her fantasies had often kept her warm at night, this
moment was infinitely better because it was *real*. So she let
everything go and fell into him, giving every bit as much as
she was getting.

Years of longing rolled through her as their lips tangled and her soft breasts molded to his hard chest, as her thighs touched his all the way down their muscled length and as her stomach—oh, glory—pushed up against his hips where she found all the evidence she needed that he was, indeed, attracted to her after all.

When she let out an involuntary moan of pure, undiluted desire, he dragged her impossibly closer and deepened their kiss until her back bumped up against the front door with a thump.

"You okay?" he said against her lips as he dropped one hand to fumble with the doorknob.

"Oh, yes," she breathed and felt him shiver as the door gave way behind her. She pulled back to look at him. "You're cold."

"Not anymore, I'm not." And then in one smooth move, he picked her up, stepped inside and kicked the door closed behind them.

The gloom of the storm made the room dim but neither of them made a move toward the light switch. Instead, Daisy wrapped her arms around Alec's neck, slanted her lips against his and boldly used her tongue to gain entry to the place that up until a few days ago, she'd only tasted in her dreams. Then she forgot all about her dreams because he was stroking her tongue with his own, sending her senses into a fabulous, frantic dance.

It wasn't until they reached the doorway that led to their rooms that he paused and drew away from her. "Your place or mine?"

She didn't hesitate. "Anywhere," she said. "Take me anywhere you want."

His eyebrows shot up. "Anywhere?"

She nodded, excitement and anticipation pooling in her stomach. "Gentleman's choice," she said, praying he'd kiss her soon to keep her lips from trembling.

"Oh, I'm no gentleman, sweetheart," he said, and his voice was husky and low, carrying with it an implication that all but set her on fire. But then, like a dark cloud marring a sunny day, his mood shifted and she saw that the desire in his eyes had been muted by concern. "You can still change your mind, Daze. We don't have to—"

"Shh," she said, then showed him exactly what was going on in her mind by silencing him with her lips.

"Good answer," he whispered and, with Daisy still in his arms, he turned right and headed to his bedroom.

He lowered her feet to the floor slowly and as every inch of her slid along every inch of him, he gave her a look so chockful of sinful possibilities that she blushed. Her heart was hammering, loud and riotous, but as soon as her toes touched the floor, she reached out and pulled his hips close. She felt the muscles in his back tense under her touch, and an incredible, shimmering excitement moved through her. He smelled wonderful and familiar, like grass and rain and something that was uniquely Alec, a deeply male scent that she knew could not come from a bottle.

Flushed with desire and longing, Daisy pulled at the bottom of his drenched polo shirt with impatient hands. He went for the hem of her sweater at the same moment but she was faster. After she pulled his shirt free, she let it fall to the floor.

He was flawless, she thought as she reached out to touch him with tentative, inexperienced fingers. A sculpted, muscled masterpiece. He felt electric beneath her exploring hands, his heart beating a hard, strong staccato against her palms that matched the chaotic rhythm of her own heart almost perfectly. She let her gaze follow the line of dark hair that trailed over his hard, six-pack stomach and disappeared into his waistband, then she let her breath out in one long, appreciative rush.

"You're beautiful, Alec," she said and let her fingers trace the line her gaze had followed only moments before. She tucked her fingertips beneath the fabric of his khakis and felt a sudden surge of power when he sucked in a sharp breath and tightened his hold on her.

"So are you," he said, his molten gaze meeting hers as he slid his hands higher and let his thumbs brush up against the swell of her aching breasts, making her nipples harden into tight, tender, yearning peaks.

The sensation he triggered with his simple touch was so exquisite she had to bite her bottom lip to keep from crying out. Even so, a little moan slipped out as he pushed her sweater up and off. The soft fabric hit the floor silently, and then Daisy stood there in her bra, trembling with anticipation and wishing for divine guidance to tell her what to do next.

Fortunately, she didn't have to do a thing. Alec reached for her and let his fingers sketch the lacy vee of her brand-new, light-blue silk demicup bra. *Oh, thank you, Virginia,* she thought, and her breath went shallow as he released the front clasp with one deft move.

As her bra fell away, a powerful tremor passed through her from head to toe, though whether from the cool air on her breasts or from the heat of his gaze, she wasn't sure. All she knew was that she thought she'd die if he didn't touch her soon, felt herself arch forward, willing him to do just that. And then he did, filling his hands with her breasts, caressing them gently and pulling and teasing her nipples with his clever fingertips.

Bliss. Daisy let her head fall back as arrows of fire shot through her body and landed achingly between her legs, warm and wet. As his attention to his task intensified, she gasped softly and dug her short fingernails into his skin, instinctively pulling him closer.

"Wait," he said as he dipped his head, let his lips slide up her neck, kissing and nipping, let his hands bury themselves in her hair.

"But I've waited for you so long already," she whispered, her voice intense.

She could hardly believe she'd said that out loud, but there it was. It was out there, and all there was to do was wait and see how he'd react.

He pulled away to look at her, his brows drawn together with confusion. The moment seemed to stretch out between them, thick as taffy. Then she saw his impossible, midnight-blue eyes darken, saw the corners of his mouth slip into an inscrutable smile. "It'll be worth the wait," he said softly as he reached for the drawstring of her shorts. "Trust me."

And she did. Trust and love and need welled up within her, and suddenly she didn't feel as if she could stand it another minute. She toed off her shoes as she went for his still-wet khakis. He peeled off her shorts as he shucked his socks. And then, after a momentary flurry of snaps and buttons and zippers, they stood naked before each other, breathing hard.

"My imagination didn't do you justice," he said, his voice reverent.

She tumbled into the depths of his eyes and forgot to be

self-conscious of her nakedness. "You imagined this? Imagined me?" she asked, breathless at the very idea.

Smiling, he pulled her close, and she thrilled at the feel of his bare skin against hers, at the feel of his warm breath fanning across her cheek. "Of course. Why do you think I have these dark circles under my eyes?"

"Good answer," she said, smiling.

He laughed then and kissed her fiercely as he backed up to the bed and pulled her down on top of him. Together they spilled onto the soft down comforter and rolled over until she lay beneath him. Alec murmured her name against her bruised and willing lips as he began to touch her everywhere, setting her skin ablaze and her heart to drumming furiously.

Her body hummed with need as she slid hungry fingers over his shoulders, down his thickly muscled back and then headed further south until she reached his perfect butt. All of it was shockingly wonderful, it was all far, far beyond her fantasies and yet it wasn't nearly enough.

"Alec," she moaned, letting instinct be her guide. "I want—" She tightened her hold on him, draped one leg around his thigh, pressed her hips closer, felt his arousal pulse against her. "Please—" She didn't know what she was asking for but whatever it was, she knew she needed it more than she needed her next breath.

Alec knew exactly what she wanted. He knew because he wanted it, too. But for reasons he couldn't possibly fathom, he desperately needed to hear her say it.

"Tell me," he murmured as his hands roamed freely over her incredible, silky skin and his tongue played with her swollen, tempting lips. "Tell me what you want," he said, cupping her sweet, round bottom and pulling her against him. His arousal pressed into the taut expanse of her stomach and he nearly came undone from wanting her. He'd been a fool. How could he have failed to see what had been sitting right there in front of him?

When she spoke, her voice was low, pleading. "I want," she began. "I want…" She kissed him deeply, thoroughly, as if she were starving and he was sustenance, and then she tried again. "Dammit," she said, and he almost smiled at the frustration in her tone. "I need *you. All of you.*"

Need. And even as his mind said, "Oh, damn," his heart started to…well, his heart started.

How long had it been since a woman had wanted him like this? When a woman's desire for him had been so tangible he could feel it surrounding him, thick and warm and wonderful? The answer descended on him like a clap of thunder. After a tiresome, endless stream of pointless encounters with beautiful but soulless women, the answer was never.

He knew this was dangerous and crazy—hell, she *drove* him crazy—but he knew he'd never wanted any woman as badly as he wanted this woman right now.

The wicked, reckless look in her eyes had his heart slamming against his ribs. It was official. The respectable, bespectacled Daisy Kincaid was history. The beautiful woman lying beneath him with the light of both innocence and sin shining in her eyes was the new and improved Daisy: bold and sexy, a gorgeous temptress.

She pulled his head down to her and renewed their kiss with a passion that sent an intense streak of pure desire sweeping through him in hard, hot waves. She moaned quietly as he abandoned her lips to burn a trail of kisses from her temple to her earlobe and down the sweet, enticing length of her neck. Oh, how he'd wanted to taste her again, he thought as her scent, heavenly and sweet, surrounded him. She sighed and her fingers played in his hair as she held him to her and, with an urgency that bordered on desperation, he moved lower, using his lips to taste her shoulders and his hands to savor her firm, round breasts.

Breathing hard, she tipped her head back against the pillows, and her fingernails grazed the hot skin of his back, leaving a shadow of her desire in their wake. His lips skimmed the smooth skin of one perfect breast before he pulled the rosy, hardened nipple into his hot, searching mouth and rolled his tongue over the sensitive bud again and again. She shook sweetly beneath his mouth and hands, moaning his name and pulling him closer, and his heart tripped and skipped and struggled to regain its natural rhythm.

He turned his attention to her other breast and deliberately took his time as he let one hand move lower, over her hard, flat stomach and down to where he slipped his fingers into the hot, wet, velvet core of her. At his touch, Daisy's hips bucked up and she began to gasp out heated little sounds of impatience.

"Alec," she whispered. "Now…"

"Soon," he answered, even though his restraint was stretched tighter than he could ever remember, tighter than he'd ever thought possible.

She whimpered in frustration when he rolled off her and reached into the nightstand to find their protection, but a moment later her bottomless dark eyes softened with understanding and appreciation for what he'd just done. And then he moved over her again and her softness yielded to him, their bodies fitting together easily, so damn easily.

She whispered his name and kneaded his back with demanding hands as he entered her slowly and teasingly and felt her stretch around him. It took every shred of self-control he had left to go slow. But then she put her lips to his neck and nipped at a sensitive spot above his collarbone and murmured her need in hushed tones, and he was lost.

He'd wanted to make it last, to let this terrible, wonderful tension spark and smolder, but he knew now he'd wanted her for too long. His control snapped and their desire collided in one amazing, blinding moment that drove him to push his way into her in one hard, heated rush.

He stilled as he met resistance and she stiffened, clutched at him, cried out softly in…was that *pain?* He tried to think, to clear his mind, but she made it all but impossible by writhing beneath him, trying to pull him more deeply inside her.

Daisy was a *virgin,* he thought, his mind a wild tangle. How could that be? "Daisy?" he choked out, reining himself in with a discipline he wouldn't have thought he could muster.

"Please, Alec," she pleaded, pushing her hips upward again. An arrow of pure pleasure pierced him as her muscles gripped him hard, pulling him deeper inside her. "Don't stop."

"Daisy…" His brain was fogged from wanting her, from the sheer paradise of being inside her, but he knew he had to make her see…something. But what was it?

"Please," she said again, pulling his head back down to hers and confusing him further with a kiss that torched his very soul. "I don't want to be an old maid."

"Old maid?" he repeated, his voice hoarse. What was she talking about? "You're only twenty-something years old—"

"But I've been wanting this." He sucked in a sharp breath when she kissed his neck, then let her lush, sweet lips flit over his stubbly chin and cheek. "*This*. With you." Her fingers curled into the hair at the nape of his neck. "Make it come true."

And then she crushed her mouth to his, thrust up once again to take him more deeply inside her, and he buckled. Nothing mattered but the miracle of this feeling, the wonder of what she was doing to him right this moment. And so he welcomed the hot tide of hunger and desire that washed over him as he followed the rhythm of her slow, seductive movements, followed her until he forgot everything he'd ever known or ever would know and just lived in that moment, inside Daisy.

When she reached the limits of her own passion, she cried out again, only this time her cry was filled with joy and awe and pleasure. Her legs shook as she convulsed around him, hard and insistent, and with his whispered name on her lips, she pulled him with her tenderly until he, too, fell over the edge and into her warm, waiting arms.

Nine

It seemed to Daisy that if she lay there very quietly, she could make this moment last long enough to memorize every detail of how it felt to have her dream come true.

Alec's marvelous, unfamiliar weight touching her everywhere; his heartbeat, loud and quick beneath her sweat-slicked cheek; the tension that continued to trickle, little by little, out of her body with each breath; her bendy, pliable limbs that seemed incapable of serious movement; the sharp, heady scent of their entwined bodies.

Each sensation, sweet and new and treasured, lingered, imprinted itself on her very soul.

She'd wanted this for so long she almost couldn't believe it had happened. But with Alec's arms encircling her, his spicy scent surrounding her and his still-labored breath playing in her hair, it was impossible to deny it. She turned her head and pressed her lips against his shoulder and felt his arms tighten around her. Then he dropped a kiss onto her unkempt curls and the gesture was so tender she had to squeeze her eyes shut to fend off the emotions that threatened to overpower her.

Her heart was still hammering like crazy when Alec rolled just far enough away to prop himself up on one elbow and demolish her with those devastating blue eyes. "Hey, you," he said.

She put on a wobbly smile and gently swept the back of her hand over his raspy cheek. "Hey, yourself," she whispered, her voice sounding oddly seductive to her own ears.

"You know, you could have told me that you..." His voice trailed off before he finished the thought, but it would've been hard to misunderstand him.

"If it'd ever come up in conversation, I'm sure I would have."

"Hmm," he said as he looked up at her. Then, with a sinful smile that might have made her fall for him if it wasn't already a done deal, he said, "We need to rethink the kinds of conversations we have, don't you agree?" as he began to draw slow, sensuous circles on her bare stomach with his fingertips.

Her heart lodged firmly in her throat. Why him? she thought as she looked over at his handsome, achingly familiar face. Why did she have to fall in love with this unavailable, unattainable, impossible man?

Lord, she thought as she bathed in his smile, if only she knew something, anything, about how to make a man fall in love with her.

"You're not mad," she said, and while she'd meant to make

it a question, the laughter in his eyes had already told her what she wanted to know.

He shook his head once, then his brows drew together over eyes suddenly filled with concern. "I didn't hurt you, did I?"

"God, no," she said on a soul deep sigh. "It was everything I imagined." *And then some.*

"You imagined this?" he asked, repeating her earlier question with a sly smile.

"Actually, wise guy," she said as she pushed him onto his back and rolled on top of him, "it was more like this." She sat up, pushed her unruly hair back from her face and struck a pose that should have made her blush but instead made her feel like the wickedest woman in the world. His intense, approving gaze swept down to her breasts, and she reveled in the passion in his eyes when he reached for her, enveloped her with his searing touch.

"What happens next?" he asked, shifting beneath her to show her the evidence of his rekindled desire.

Renewed excitement flooded every fiber of her being, along with a surge of power and confidence she'd never dreamed she'd experience. She lifted herself off him, just high enough to take the tip of his erection inside her. "This happens next," she said softly, and his expression went from lazy to intense in an instant as she slowly, slowly took him all in.

He grasped her hips and his fingers were strong and sure as he helped guide her down over every splendid inch of him. "I love the way your mind works," he said on a groan torn from deep inside.

And I love you, she thought, biting her lip to keep from saying it out loud. *I love you enough to take whatever piece of you that you'll share with me.*

Then they began to move, body to body, soul to soul, in an ancient rhythm that bound them, made them one. Together, with frantic hands and inquisitive lips and tender words, they climbed higher, impossibly higher, to a place so exquisite, she shivered at the sweet miracle of it.

And then, as they found their release in an explosive melding of minds and bodies and souls, Daisy Kincaid's reality finally, blissfully, eclipsed her fantasies.

Alec had been pretty busy the last few months and hadn't quite gotten in all the workouts he should have and right about now—boy, oh, boy—could he feel it.

His shoulders ached, he had a tic in his neck, and his back was pinging somewhere in the middle of his shoulder blades—probably from that acrobatic thing he and Daisy had done around three in the morning when she'd woken him up with a single, seductive touch of her hand to a place on his body that just couldn't say no.

But his twinges and pains weren't really important. All that really mattered was that they'd had one hell of a night.

He smiled as he tightened his arm around Daisy's slim waist and tugged her closer. It was nice the way her back pressed up to the front of his body, her contours molding to his hardened planes with ease. She was warm and soft and smelled, as always, like fresh-baked cookies. He sucked in a deep breath and thought, "I could really get used to this," and then he snapped his eyes open in surprise.

Blinding sunlight filled the room, birds sang outside on the patio, the clock ticked loudly on the nightstand—and Alec Mackenzie had just woken up with a woman in his arms for the first time in his life.

Oh, he'd gone to bed with women, lots of them. But waking up with them? That was much too intimate. Alec had always been careful not to form any close bonds with the women he dated. And yet here he was, spooning with Daisy as if it was the most natural thing in the world. *Spooning*. He'd never even said that *word* before, not even to himself.

This was not good, he thought, forcing himself not to jump away from her. Next thing he knew, he'd be telling her all about his pitiful, lonely childhood and crying in her arms like men did in those silly romantic chick flicks.

Daisy was dangerous. He didn't know what it was about her, but she's was definitely messing with his mind. Never before had a woman occupied his thoughts this way, never had a woman made his body react just from thinking about her, never had a woman captivated him so completely that he loathed every minute he couldn't be with her.

Yes, she was dangerous. Dangerous to his peace of mind, dangerous to his freedom and dangerous to the carefully constructed rules of the game by which he played. Because she was the kind of woman who dreamed of—and, apparently, could even make someone like him think of—the dreaded triad of love and marriage and children.

And that made him want to jump in a helicopter, go home and plunge himself back into his familiar life, because one thing he was sure of was that he was never going to get married. The disastrous sham of a union that his parents had dragged him through was enough for him to swear it off, but he also had some pretty impressive national statistics on his side. The failure of one in two marriages spelled *don't bother* to Alec.

But he and Daisy were never going to get that far. She

would realize that he was a terminal bachelor and that he was never going to change and she'd leave him. He knew she was capable of it—hell, she'd bailed on him once already when she'd quit without warning. And while the short-lived nature of his relationships didn't normally bother him, something told him that this time he wouldn't be taking it in stride.

Warm and silky, Daisy murmured something and laughed softly in her sleep, then wiggled her butt up against the danger zone and his temperature spiked to critical levels. What he wanted to do was wake her and continue what they'd started last night. She was sweet and lush and just so damned tempting, but he resisted, dropped a kiss onto her velvety shoulder and eased away from her.

As he pulled on a pair of jeans, he noticed a beam of sunlight streaking across the floor from window to bed, reminding him that last night's storm was over. Now all he had to do, he thought as he crept out of the room, was deal with the storm that raged inside him.

Daisy's cat joined him in the hallway and raced him to the kitchenette, then meowed insistently as it wound its furry body around Alec's ankles.

"What?" he asked the cat in a voice that clearly said, "Get the hell away from me, furball."

But the cat merely looked up at him with its big, round, sincere cat eyes and blinked.

Sighing, Alec opened a can of food for the little pest and the cat thanked him by turning its back on him and attacking its breakfast with gusto. Alec snorted in disgust. Why did women love their cats so much? he wondered. Now, dogs on the other hand…dogs were more like people. Cats were always acting like they knew a secret or something. It was annoying.

Alec opened the cabinets and stared blindly at the contents, lost in thoughts of Daisy. He thought about how their bodies fit together perfectly, how she sounded when she came apart in his hands, how she'd wanted him to be the first one for her. And then he thought about how knowing all that was going to make it so much harder to end this thing.

Because no matter how tempting, sexy, smart, sweet, fun…anyway, it didn't matter. This would end. It always did. Alec didn't do forever and it was better to lay his cards on the table right now. Because this time he had a horrible feeling that he had something to lose.

He sighed and leaned on the cabinet door while the cat licked its paws rapturously. At least he could make Daisy breakfast. And maybe, just maybe, if he didn't char the toast to a cinder and made her a decent cup of joe, she might not kill him for what he was about to tell her.

Something was burning.

Daisy sat up in bed—not her own bed, she remembered as she saw Alec's clothes hanging in the closet—and was just about to throw her legs over the side to go investigate when she heard him coming down the hallway.

She clutched the sheet to her naked body. *Damn.* She'd never done a morning after. Did he regret what they'd done? And speaking of that, did she? She checked in with herself quickly and realized that no, she absolutely didn't. So, acting on instinct, she fell back against the pillows and buried herself in the covers and willed her heart to slow down so she could feign sleep.

Oh, dear. Oh, dear. Oh, dear, she thought as she heard him come into the room and bang into the dresser.

"Damn," he whispered fiercely, and she popped one eye open to see him with a tray in one hand, the toe he'd just mangled in the other. Naked from the waist up, he looked like a hunky slice of heaven. Yummy, she thought, and then the whole night flooded back, from the first kiss to the hot, spiraling climax she'd had in the wee hours as the moonlight had sifted through the shutters.

As if he could hear her thoughts, Alec looked over at her and she slammed her eye shut and resumed playing possum.

"Daze," he called quietly, and the mattress tipped to one side under his weight when he sat down. "Daisy, wake up."

Her heart flip-flopped hard in her chest. She cracked her eye open again and saw him sitting there, carrying the tray that held two coffee cups and a plate with some blackened toast.

"Morning," he said, smiling.

She faked a stretch and smiled back. "Morning." He looked so good it almost hurt.

He held the tray aloft. "Here it is. Everything I know how to cook."

She sat up, carefully tucking the sheet under her arms to cover herself. "Looks—" she eyeballed the black toast "—interesting."

He set the tray down on the comforter and with a brief, appreciative glance at her sheet-clad breasts, he handed her a cup of coffee. "I think I did the coffee right."

She sipped…and by sheer will alone managed not to choke. And not just because it was the worst coffee she'd ever tasted—although it was—but because somehow the man who was so clueless he didn't even know she'd been in love with him for the past year knew that she took her coffee black with two sugars.

In that moment, her crush-turned-love deepened impossibly further. She wanted to cry.

"Delicious," she said with a watery smile.

He narrowed his eyes in suspicion, took a drink from his own cup and grimaced. "Liar."

And just like that, the spell was broken. She laughed. "It was the thought," she said.

He smiled as he took the cup from her and set the tray and its contents aside. But then his demeanor grew more serious.

"What?" she asked after a long moment had passed.

He looked deeply into her eyes, as if he was memorizing her for a test. "I have a question for you," he said.

Her imagination kick-started and took off at a hundred miles an hour. Last night was a mistake. Not disclosing her virgin status had been a bad idea. She was fired. Worse, he still wanted her to stay after this job was done. "Uh, okay," she said, twisting her hands in her lap.

"What happened to your glasses?"

"What?" she asked, incredulous. "Why?"

"You used to wear them all the time."

"We-ell," she stalled. "I really only need them for reading."

He reached out and dragged a thumb across her cheek. "I like you better without them."

"Thank you," she said, suddenly shy. Then she laughed out loud.

He raised an eyebrow in question. "What?"

"I thought you were going to tell me that last night was a mistake."

The serious look on his face grew more serious.

"Oh," she said and her smile died. "I guess you were getting around to that."

He shook his head but she knew he was lying. "It wasn't a mistake," he said. An inscrutable smile lit his features for a moment before he went on. "It was amazing. Wheels-off, howl-at-the-moon, amazing." Then he shook his head again. "But you know me, the kind of guy I am. That's not going to change, Daisy."

She couldn't be absolutely sure because this was all pretty new to her, but this sounded very much like he was trying to let her down easy. Dread filled all the places inside her that had been filled with happiness a few minutes earlier. "I don't remember asking you to change."

"No, you didn't but—"

"I'm a big girl, remember? I make my own choices." She'd waited too long for this to happen. She wasn't going down without a fight, dammit. "Besides, I know exactly who you are."

His hand moved reflexively and she thought he might reach out to touch her again but then he let his arm drop to his side. "You think you do but you—"

"Alec, wake up." She leaned forward and covered his hand with hers. "Who knows you better than I do?"

He sucked in a big breath, let it out. She bit her lip, waited for him to deliver the whopper he'd just tried to swallow. "Daze, you want…hell, you deserve more than I have to give."

She did. She wanted everything. The whole matrimonial enchilada. But last night—sometime between act of passion number one and act of passion number nine—she'd decided that she could live with the fact that she wasn't going to get that from him. She could and she would.

Of course, there was always the possibility that he would fall in love with her…

Ah, there it was, she thought as she grabbed his hand and pulled him down next to her. Her optimism, right back where it belonged. She slipped her arms around his neck and tipped her head to whisper in his ear, "I know what I want." She nipped at his earlobe and he sucked in a breath and then she said, very softly, "Thank you for hiring me back, Alec." *Nibble.* "For wanting me here with you." *Nibble.* "I wouldn't have missed this for the world."

He stiffened in her arms for a beat, so she nibbled on his ear some more and let her lips play around a sensitive spot on his neck she'd found last night. *C'mon, give it up, Mackenzie.*

Alec groaned and said, "Ah, hell," and after that it only took a second for him to roll her beneath him and a second more for him to find her lips and urge their kiss to an immoral, feverish place that had him crushing his mouth against hers, bruising her lips in a way that sent her mind spinning and her heart soaring. He tossed away the sheet that separated them, and the absolute perfection of his skin against hers made her sigh into his mouth, made her rejoice all over again that fate had seen fit to make this magnificent man her first.

His strong, callused hand slipped down over her breast and cupped it gently while he used his thumb to tease her nipple into a hard, aching peak. Then he took her into his mouth and pulled gently, again and again, and she moaned as a thick, warm flush of pleasure slipped down her body and pooled between her trembling legs.

Her skin burned beneath his hand as he moved down her body, caressing and stroking across her stomach, then lower until he found her, wet and ready. and slid his fingers inside her. She clutched the sheets in her fists and arched up to meet him, then she bit down hard on her lower lip when she felt his breath, hot and fluid, on her skin as he used his lips to follow the same path his hand had just taken.

Oh, yes, she thought as he lifted her to him with clever, urgent hands and used his tongue and mouth to take her, thrashing and moaning and begging, to the very boundary of her being. She buried her hands in his dark hair and let the waves of sheer pleasure take her, pulling her down, deeper and deeper, until finally a wondrous, delicious release seized her and swept her away in one fast, furious, unstoppable surge.

He smiled down at her as he stripped off his jeans and then, with his breathing ragged and reckless in her ear, he entered her while her body still vibrated with sweet aftershocks. She took him, all of him, took him gratefully, and loved that he filled her so completely.

And then she forgot to think at all as they began to move as one, and her body and her heart opened impossibly further to him. Their pleasure deepened and swirled and intensified and then finally he, too, surrendered, crying out her name with one last thrust, taking her with him to a place she knew in her heart she'd only ever be able to find again in his arms.

Daisy tore the concrete contractor's bid out of the fax machine, read through it quickly, initialed her approval and fed it right back into the machine. While the pages zoomed through the ether, she updated her costs spreadsheet, printed a copy and laid it on Alec's desk.

Busy did not begin to describe the last few days, she thought as she absently began straightening his messy desk.

Monday morning, right after they'd gotten out of the shower—another lovely, erotic, heart-stopping first for her—a local contractor they'd hired to do some framing had knocked on the door and soon after that the phone had begun ringing, packages had started arriving, meetings had started happening.

The Santa Margarita job had officially begun.

It had taken no time at all for Alec and Daisy to settle into a routine. When it came to work, they were a well-oiled machine. Daisy handled everything behind the scenes—the bids, the books, the orders, the deliveries, phones, blueprints, permits and, of course, her specialty—inspectors. Alec handled design and everything that happened on-site, from dealing with contractors to making sure that no one tried to stick them with a truckload of knotted, warped boards. And while this division of labor worked well and made good sense, the downside was that it kept them apart a great deal of the day.

Fortunately, they were both passionately committed to making the most of their nights.

And oh, the nights, Daisy thought as she gathered up the pencils he'd left strewn about the table and put them all into the empty cup where they belonged. They'd been the most amazing three nights of Daisy's life. She felt her face flush when she thought about how bold she'd become so quickly, how much time she'd made up for in Alec's arms.

The only problem was that each caress, each moan and gasp and overwhelming climax made her fall harder and more hopelessly in love. And with that realization came the knowledge that when the time came, she was going to have one hell of a time letting him go.

The phone rang, dragging her back to Thursday, day six of the ninety or so she'd spend here on Santa Margarita, making love with the man who was most definitely going to break her heart.

"Mackenzie," she said into the receiver as she dropped into Alec's desk chair.

"Kincaid," Alec said with mock gravity, his low, sexy voice causing her blood to pop in her veins.

Her heart rate kicked up to a cha-cha beat. "You on your way home?"

"As fast as this damn cart will take me. You okay?"

"Yes." How domestic this all sounded, she thought, while it was anything but. For one crazy second, she considered telling him that she loved him. That, in spite of what she'd said, she was dreading the day she was going to lose him. "It's been a busy day." *Coward.*

"Hey, if I haven't told you already," he said, concern heavy in his voice, "you're doing an amazing job. I don't know how I would be handling this without you."

"Thanks, Alec." She loved the job. In fact, staying busy all day was the only thing that kept her mind off their future—or lack thereof.

"I have an idea," he said, then quickly added, "and I'm still the boss, so you can't say no."

She smiled, thinking how much their relationship had changed in recent days. "What's your idea, boss?" she asked, leaning on the final word.

"Ohh, I like that," he said, and she could almost see him stroking a nonexistent villain's beard. "Subservience. Hmm. That gives me another idea…"

"Stick to the first idea, Snidely Whiplash."

"Oh, that." He managed to inject disappointment into the simple words. "What was that again?"

"Alec…"

"Take an hour and treat yourself to something at the spa over on Catalina Lane."

"Thanks, but there's so much to do—"

"Did I mention I was the boss?"

"You did mention that, yes," she said, her tone dry.

"Then go on. Chop, chop. No dinner meeting tonight so I'll pick something up."

"I don't know," she began.

"I'm having a hard time being this nice," he said, "so the offer expires in exactly ten seconds. Nine. Eight. Seven. Six—"

"Okay," she said as she reached for her purse.

"And, Daisy?"

"Yeah?"

"Don't get an overhaul. I like you just the way you are."

Damn him.

Alec took a long pull on a tall beer and collapsed onto the suite's overstuffed couch. Something was definitely wrong. He was sure of it because he was starting to do things that only jerky, sensitive, New-Age guys did.

For starters, he'd been calling Daisy all day long lately— always under the guise of talking about work, but he knew he just wanted to hear her voice. Tonight he'd even called her on the way home—like a husband, for pity's sake. Then he'd offered to pick up dinner, which wouldn't have been a big deal except that he'd made it a big deal by calling the chef at *Pitcairn* and bribing her to whip up a special menu. Then he'd spent the next hour running all over town picking stuff up, making nice with the surly proprietor òf the wine shop and telling flagrant lies to the girls at the bakery who'd already closed up for the night.

All in all, he was definitely having an out-of-body experience.

A sigh loud enough to wake Daisy's cat didn't make him feel any better, either. He had to admit it, he thought as the cat got up, stretched his back into a perfect Halloween cat arch and settled down to lick one soft paw. He wanted Daisy the way he'd never wanted any woman. Not in a forever kind of way, of course, but in ways that alarmed him and ways that intrigued him and ways that made him feel like he'd already lost his freaking mind.

He looked over at Daisy's neatly ordered desk and all the familiar things she'd laid out on its surface—coffee cups filled with pens, a rack that held her color-coded folders, a stack of Post-its, a framed photo of her with her late mother. It struck him as ironic that all of that was so predictable while the woman herself had turned out to be anything but.

The cat—whose name was Barney or something—chose that moment to give him one of those cat looks that said, "You don't like me so I'm going to love you up until you start sneezing," and promptly jumped onto Alec's lap.

"Aw, c'mon," Alec said, holding his arms away from the cat in hopes it would get the hint.

It didn't. It just turned in a dozen tiny circles, curled up into a neat yellow ball right there on his legs and began to purr. Loudly.

Alec tried to harden his heart against the furry monster, but when he looked down at the contentment on the cat's face, he gave up. "All right. But don't make this a habit."

Barney just blinked and purred louder. Then he dropped his head down on his front paws and exhaled with a little wheeze.

"You got a pretty good gig here, don't you?" he asked as he began to scratch the cat behind the ears absently. "Eat. Sleep. Love. The end."

Barney let out a little *snore-snuffle* combo. "Maybe I'll take a page out of your book, Barney. Maybe I'll try being domesticated for a while." Alec took another swig of his beer. "I sure am tempted."

"I thought you and cats didn't get along."

Startled, Alec coughed and gagged as he twisted around in his seat. "Daisy," he said as he sat up straight, ejecting the cat in the process. "How long have you been standing there?"

"Long enough to know that you weren't paying attention when I told you his name was Bam Bam."

"I knew it was one of the Flintstones."

"Rubbles."

"Whatever."

Daisy stood in the doorway, her curvy figure silhouetted by the orange-purple glow of the sun's dying light behind her. A warm breeze had slipped in with her, bringing with it the unique island scents of sand and sea and passion.

She stepped inside and shut the door and he saw a tempting glimpse of her flat stomach beneath her cropped red shirt, a long, enticing stretch of her tanned legs below an abbreviated denim skirt and a bad girl's smile lighting up her pretty face.

His throat went bone dry.

"What's for dinner, honey?" she asked, teasing him as she walked toward him, her hips swaying with each graceful step.

Heat sizzled in his veins. How was he supposed to resist thinking what it would be like to come home to this every night, when he'd had more fun in the last five days than he'd had in the previous five years?

"Just a little something I threw together." He put down his beer and stood. "Come on," he said, and took her hand and led her through the French doors and out onto the patio where he'd laid out a red-checked tablecloth and the most decadent spread he could muster on such short notice.

Daisy didn't say a thing. She just nibbled on her bottom lip. When she looked up at him, her eyes were suspiciously shiny. "You did this for me?"

"Only the best for you," he said as he pulled out a chair for her. *Except me. I'm not the best thing for you but, heaven help me, I can't seem to stay away.*

She spread a napkin out on her lap and chewed a little harder on her lip. "This is so sweet."

Sweet, he thought. Only sensitive, New-Age guys were sweet. *Damn.*

"Don't worry," he said with a wink as he took a seat across from her. "I'll make up for the sweetness with a little bit of sin later, I promise."

And he was a man of his word. After they ate the oysters on the half shell and the French bean salad with sea scallops and the salmon filet with goat cheese gratin and the Tahitian vanilla crème brûlée, he took her to bed and showed her that even newly minted, sensitive, New-Age guys could turn wicked when they wanted someone the way he wanted her.

Ten

"Hello?" Even with the bathroom door between them, Daisy could hear the annoyance in Alec's voice.

She peered into the mirror and nearly jabbed the mascara wand into her eye. "Almost ready," she sang out. Goodness, this whole girly thing took a long time. Hair, makeup, clothes, lingerie and, oh, Lord, *these shoes,* she thought as she reached down and adjusted one strappy heel. So damned uncomfortable.

She threw some of the cosmetics in her tiny bag and put on dangly crystal earrings, then adjusted her dress, sucked in her cheeks and struck a pose à la Marilyn Monroe.

"Pathetic, Kincaid," she said to her reflection. "You look like a tomboy dressed up like a girl."

"Daisy," he said, and she could almost hear him looking at his watch. "Tell me the truth. Are we going somewhere tonight or—"

Daisy yanked open the door and tried to stand still as Alec perused her with a gaze so hungry and appreciative she felt like she was vibrating beneath the force of it. She distracted herself by checking him out just as thoroughly. He looked gorgeous in his tuxedo, like Cary Grant with a touch of Jimmy Stewart thrown in for flavor.

"Wow," he said finally.

She smiled, relaxed, smoothed the fabric of her black satin, bias-cut, low-cut glamour gown over her hips. "You like?"

"Oh, baby," he said, reaching for her, pulling her into his arms, bending her around the hand he laid at the small of her back. "Me like." Then he kissed her with such attention to detail that she couldn't catch her breath. In the end she had no choice but to believe that she looked pretty damned good.

"Alec?" she gasped against his consuming lips, her heart pounding hard and furious. "Are we going somewhere tonight or—"

"I haven't decided. What do you have on under that dress?"

"White cotton granny panties and a sports bra."

"Oh," he moaned. "I love it when you talk dirty."

She laughed and smacked him on the arm before pulling reluctantly out of his embrace. "Come on. We're late."

"No one will notice if we don't show."

"At a thousand-dollar-a-plate benefit?"

"Okay," he conceded, smiling like the devil. "The caterer will notice."

She grabbed his shoulders, turned him toward the door and pushed. "Chop, chop," she said and he obeyed.

With the darkening sunset guiding their way, they walked

hand in hand to Paloma's largest venue, the Cosmopolitan Ballroom, to attend a benefit for Virginia's pet charity, the Santa Margarita Trust. As they walked, they passed legions of Saturday night revelers on the gas lamp lit sidewalks. But Daisy and Alec were so intent on talking, laughing and sometimes moving into the shadows to grope each other that they hardly noticed.

After a full week of working together by day and making love by night, Daisy could honestly say she'd never been happier. Things that had been missing her entire adult life—a sense of belonging, of being needed and desired and feminine—were now hers in spades. Her relationship with Alec was a big part of the changes in her, but she could also credit her new job responsibilities for giving her confidence and a sense of purpose. The only speed bump on her horizon was that it was all going to end long before she was ready.

Soon the Ballroom loomed up before them, a huge and imposing marble structure that housed, among other things, a movie theater, a bowling alley, a casino and a museum. Before they headed for the main entrance, they circled the building and Alec told her what he knew about its history, recounting with awe the engineering feats that made the hundred-year-old building legendary among architects.

She smiled up at him, loving his intelligence and wit and passion for his work. Loving him.

"I'm sorry," he said when it was clear she'd drifted away somewhere. "This must be dull as all hell."

She shook her head. "I'm on the edge of my seat," she said and he kissed her and called her a liar in a fond voice before guiding her into the building with a strong hand at the small of her back.

Virginia and Joseph greeted them warmly and escorted them to their table. The sound of a live orchestra was filling the huge room with rich, gorgeous melodies as the guests mingled and waited for the dinner to commence. Slowly couples began to wander out onto the ballroom floor.

Alec held out a hand in invitation. "What do you say?"

"Why not," she said, and thought, *Thank you, Arthur Murray,* as Alec led the way.

He took her in his arms and held her so close she could feel him breathing. Her heart thumped against his ribs, his pulse beat hard against her cheek. She wished she had some wood she could knock on because she couldn't stop thinking that her fantasies were working out just fine.

When dinner was announced, they returned to the table. Business associates and friends of the Baldwins had rounded out their table, leaving just one empty seat next to Alec.

The dinner passed in a blur of conversation and wine and exquisite food and high spirits. The ornate chandeliers above them cast prisms of light on the china and crystal and silver on the table, making Daisy think whimsically that she'd fallen into a sparkling fairyland. Occasionally Alec would reach for her hand under the table and Daisy's breath would hitch as he played with her fingers or traced a pattern on her palm, and all the while he'd carry on a passionate discussion with one of their table mates about design or architecture or history.

Her heart hurt just looking at him, but the pain was well worth the return. She squeezed his hand, smiled at her good fortune and loved him just a tiny bit more.

Alec looked over at Daisy, saw the emotion in her eyes. He leaned over to whisper in her ear, "You okay?"

She was nodded and whispered, "I'm wonderful," and something powerful clutched at his chest when her hand trembled in his.

"I've been meaning to tell you something," he said and he smiled as her brows drew together in a frown. "You look stunning."

And she did, he thought as she smiled at him, clearly pleased. She was like one long, slim column of black magic, from her unruly curls that had been partially tamed into a sophisticated style to her toes which had been painted a very tempting ruby red. Later, he thought, he looked forward to finding out what she really was wearing underneath that incredible, sexy dress.

He looked into her velvet-brown eyes, then his gaze fell to the lush, red lips he couldn't wait to kiss and he realized it was time to go. She gazed back at him, a knowing smile curving her lips, and he experienced a moment of sheer expectation that shook him to the roots of his being.

It was in that perfect moment that she leaned over and whispered into his ear, "Let's go home now."

They stood and thanked their hosts for a lovely evening and tried not to seem too anxious to leave. Virginia seemed dismayed at their early departure and begged for a private word with Daisy, who reluctantly walked away with the woman, casting a longing glance over her shoulder at him. He shot her an understanding grin and took his seat again.

It was only a moment later when a soft, bejeweled hand touched him lightly on the shoulder. He turned, smile still in place…and then his good mood died.

"Hello, Alec," his mother said, her face composed into the same serene mask she'd been wearing all his life.

He cast one accusing glance at Joseph, who suddenly seemed engrossed in the tin tiles on the lofty ceiling. "Barbara," Alec said simply. "What are you doing here?"

"Well," she said as she slipped into the empty seat beside him. "I could tell you it's a wonderful coincidence."

"But it's not."

"No. The Baldwins told me you were here and I begged an invitation."

"That was nice of them," Alec said with another hard glance at Joseph.

"Yes," she said as she leaned toward him. "I've been trying to get in touch with you for quite some time. I want to talk to you."

He sat there, impassive beneath her waiting stare.

She cleared her throat and smoothed her perfectly done hair. "Can we go somewhere…?"

"No. I'm here with someone," he said, looking around for Daisy. When he found her with Virginia several yards away, she was looking back at him with her brow furrowed, her eyes worried.

"Is that Daisy?" Barbara asked, and he was startled for a moment until he remembered that the Baldwins were blabbermouths.

"Yes," he said, never taking his eyes off Daisy.

"I'd love to meet her. It looks like she makes you very happy."

"We were just on our way out," he said, hoping to cut this charade short. "So maybe another time—"

She dropped a hand onto his arm to stop him. "I want to apologize, Alec."

Apologize? His mother wanted to apologize? He swiveled his gaze toward her. "For what?"

She glanced at the other guests seated around the table and then, apparently satisfied that they had good manners enough to mind their own business, she took a deep breath. "For being the world's worst mother," she said in a rush of hushed words. "For leaving you with nannies while I went to Europe, for sending you to boarding school, for never coming to your crew races or your graduations or awards ceremonies. For never, ever being there when you needed me."

Barbara closed her eyes for a moment. When she opened them again, she looked like she might cry, which was impossible because his mother never cried. Ever.

"I can still remember the look on your face," she whispered, "when I told you I was going to miss the party for your seventh birthday. In my mind, I can still see the smudge of dirt on your cheek and the little scrape on your forehead. And I can still see your sadness and how hard you tried to fight back the tears. I'll never forgive myself for that, Alec." She gripped his arm a little tighter. "But I hope someday you can."

Alec felt the old anger flare bright and hot inside him. He was the only child of his parents' farce of a marriage. Once they'd divorced, he'd had little contact with his disinterested father and had seen the door close behind his beloved mother more often than not as she left for parties and trips and, later, for the never-ending work at the auction houses. As an adult, he'd opted out of relationships with both of them. Until a few years ago, it seemed to work for everybody.

Apparently, his mother had suddenly had an attack of conscience. About thirty-five years too late.

He stared into her eyes, the same eyes he saw every morning when he looked into the mirror. And for one brief moment he let himself wonder what it would have been like to be a part of a real family, to live with people who loved him, people he could count on. He'd thought about it often as a child, but never as an adult…until recently, anyway. He cast another glance at Daisy, then turned back to his mother.

"What happened?" he asked. "What's bringing this on now?"

She looked down and flipped her slim, expensive purse around in her hands for a moment. "I sold my business a few months back," she said and her voice was low and measured, calmer than he remembered. "Now that I have more time on my hands, I can see that I've been running in circles for decades. I can see that I've treated work like my family and my family like work." She looked up, her eyes glistening, and her composed façade began to crumble. "In the process, Alec, I'm afraid I missed out on one of life's greatest relationships."

He stared hard at her, blinked away an itch behind his eyes. "Well, thank you for the apology," he said when he found his voice. "But I'm not sure what else to say."

She reached out and squeezed his arm again, and he looked down at her hand, still cool and smooth just as he remembered. "You don't have to say anything now. But maybe we can have dinner later this week."

"I don't know—"

"I know you're busy," she said, and patted him awkwardly. "I'm staying with the Baldwins for a while. You can find me there."

When Virginia and Daisy came back to the table a few minutes later, introductions were made, desserts were enjoyed, coffee was consumed. Later, when everyone moved to the casino's gaming rooms to gamble away enough money to fill the coffers of Virginia Baldwin's pet charity for another year, Alec and Daisy quietly made their exit.

"Virginia told me about why your mother came here," Daisy said as soon as they stepped out into the cool, damp night air. "Are you okay?"

"Of course," he answered but he wasn't sure it was true. In fact, his mother's apology had triggered something more troubling, something that was making him think that his relationship with Daisy wasn't going to be as easy to walk away from as he'd planned. "Sort of a too-little, too-late thing as far as I'm concerned." As they strolled along the boardwalk, he took her hand in his, twining his fingers around her long, graceful ones.

"Oh," she said. It was only one word, one syllable, but he couldn't fail to notice that it conveyed disappointment.

"I don't need my mommy anymore," he said, and his voice was a bit too loud amidst the dinging buoys and the lapping waves and the soft music of the Paloma harbor. "But I'm glad she got it off her chest."

She stroked his thumb with her own. "You know what, Alec? This is that arm's length thing again."

"Oh, God," he groaned.

"And I understand why you do it," she said, ignoring him. "I really do. But this is your mother."

"She hasn't been much of a mom. Ask her. She'll tell you."

"Life is terribly short, Alec. And fickle." She paused and was quiet for a while before she said, "You never know how long someone you love will stick around."

She grew silent after that, and he was pretty sure he knew where her thoughts had gone. She'd lost her mother long ago, but the pain was still fresh in her voice.

He lifted her hand to his lips as they walked. "Okay, Daze.

I'll accept her invitation and have dinner with her. You can even come along if you want. Make sure I behave myself."

"Oh, no," she said, and her voice was infinitely lighter than it had been just a minute earlier. "You need this time alone with her so she can get to know her marvelous son."

He smiled into the sweet, quiet darkness that surrounded them and pulled her closer to his side. "You like me, don't you?"

She laid her cheek against him and sighed. "It's true," she said. "I really do."

They walked back to the hotel, laughing softly in the moonlight and whispering the wicked deeds they had planned for each other when they were alone. But when they got back to their room and Alec took Daisy into his arms, felt her soft skin against his and breathed her sweet scent, wickedness was the last thing on his mind.

All he could think of as he took her mouth in the lightest of kisses was that he was, without a doubt, happier than he had ever been in his life.

"Amazing," he said, pulling back to see her.

She smiled up at him and nodded and he felt his heart twinge one last time before it expanded and grew heavy with the weight of his overwhelming need for her.

He wanted to tell her something that would make her understand how he felt, to share the tremendous burden of this unfamiliar sensation. But then she dug her fingers into his hair, pulled him closer and kissed him with an intensity that shook him. The heaviness lifted, and all that was left was her, there in his arms.

He fell into her and melted into her pure, incredible heat before he scooped her up in his arms and laid her gently onto the bed. He sank down beside her, traced a teasing line down the side of her body with his fingertips and asked, "Anything you need?"

"Anything?" she asked, her expression growing serious.

Then it was his turn to get serious. "I can't think of anything I wouldn't do for you, sweetheart," he said, rolling just far enough away to gain access to her full, round breasts, to the warm skin of her stomach, to the hot, wet heat at the vee of her thighs.

As his hand moved over every smooth curve of her body, he could feel her trembling, could feel the vibration moving between them, sweet and seductive and unstoppable. And then she moaned, begged for more and he gave it, even as his own arousal pooled low and deep in his stomach like a wave of desire, pulling him under its powerful force.

She gasped as he stroked her, arched into his hand like a contented cat, twisted her hips to invite him further inside. "I want you right…here. Don't stop," she begged as his fingers played in her damp curls, then dipped in again and again to explore her sensual folds.

"I won't—"

"Ever," she finished.

"Ever," he agreed, and then she rolled on top of him, took him inside her, and it was his turn to beg her to stay right where she was, doing exactly as she was doing.

He whispered his need for her in gasping, halting, incomprehensible words, and she sighed in a kind of surrender before she leaned over and kissed him, using her tongue to tease and soothe in turns as she moved and rocked, making the world spin around them with the exquisite motion of her body on his.

The tension built, higher and higher, gathering in his muscles and his mind and his heart, until every fiber of him reached out to the very essence of her. Then, suddenly, she straightened above him and he saw her face, eyes closed, lips parted, brow furrowed. Lord, what was this feeling? he thought as he let his hands roam down over her delicious, insanely sweet body to the delicate curve of her hips, helped guide their rhythm to an intense, spiraling, endlessly perfect place until finally, blissfully, she contracted around him, cried out his name in a sound of anguish, of hope, ecstasy and love.

Her release exploded inside him, and everything within him that yearned for her rolled and swelled and burst into countless tiny, sparkling fragments. He gasped, cried out her name, then thrust up one more time, taking her to the end of herself, to the end of him, to an unspoiled place where they could dwell together for as long as the fates allowed.

Daisy was fantasizing again.

She knew it wasn't good for her peace of mind, but she couldn't help herself. Somewhere between slipping into that slinky dress and slipping between the soft, cool sheets with Alec last night, something…no, *everything* had changed between them. And against her better judgment, she now found herself thinking that this thing with Alec might just work out, that Alec's feelings for her might be deepening to the point where he might be ready to let her inside his traditional arm's length.

But that was just a fantasy, she reminded herself as she sat up, stretched and yawned. And her fantasies had never done her any favors in the past, so she struggled back to reality and the events that were happening in the real world. Here. Safely outside her overactive imagination.

She glanced at the clock and realized with a start that Alec had left to visit the job sites over an hour ago. And that meant that Daisy only had thirty minutes to get ready and meet Nikki at the dock.

Their receptionist, for all her gossipy ways, was a very nice girl. In fact, she'd been the first to volunteer to deliver a handful of overnight packages that had been shipped to the main office by mistake, which saved them both the cost and delay of having them redelivered.

Daisy didn't want to be late, so she showered and dressed and ran down to the dock. She got there just in time to hear the ferry's horn as it arrived. Nikki was one of the first people to get off the boat and she didn't look as if she'd fared particularly well on the two-hour trip. When Nikki reached the top of the gangplank, Daisy could see that her knuckles were white where they clutched the packages, that her skin was an unhealthy mix of yellow and green, that her cropped red hair looked as if she'd pulled her fingers through it about a thousand times.

Daisy gave her a light hug when she stepped onto terra firma. "You okay?" Daisy asked even though she could see the answer in the way Nikki swallowed repeatedly, her jaw pumping and grinding.

"God, no," she said, and Daisy led the way back to the hotel and got Nikki settled into a chaise lounge on the patio with a cup of Earl Grey tea. While Nikki recuperated, Daisy opened the packages and dealt with their contents, then puttered around the office a bit before returning to check on her guest.

"Thank goodness that's passed," Nikki said, looking pinker and healthier than she had earlier.

Daisy laughed. "Thanks for making the trip." She looked out over the harbor. "It's worth it just for this view, isn't it?"

"It's gorgeous," Nikki said, then immediately leaned in for the kill. "So tell me. How are you and Mr. Mackenzie doing?"

Daisy paused for a moment, then lasered her gaze on Nikki. "What do you mean exactly?"

Nikki shrugged to convey the innocence of her question. Daisy had seen her do it a million times. It was the steely glint in her eyes that gave her away. "I only meant that you guys seemed a little snippety with each other before you left."

Daisy relaxed. Only she and Alec knew what had transpired since then. Their secret was safe from little Miss Scuttlebutt for now.

"And I guess," Nikki went on with another quick shrug, "everyone was just wondering how you felt about the client forcing him to hire you back."

Forcing... Daisy's smile staggered. "I'm sorry," she said finally. "What was that?"

"You know," Nikki said with a dismissive wave. "Joseph Baldwin called and you were gone and he told Mr. Mackenzie that he had to hire you back or no contract." Nikki looked out over the harbor and the part of town they could see from their patio. "Word has it Mr. Mackenzie fought it like a wild man, but I bet he's glad he knuckled under now. I hear the client's really happy with the firm. And this place is great."

"Yes, it is," Daisy agreed mechanically as she tried to put order to her chaotic thoughts, to understand why she suddenly felt so cold.

"Anyway," Nikki went on, oblivious to Daisy's distress.

"The office grapevine is buzzing about this job being a real make-it-or-break-it thing for Mackenzie professionally so he's real lucky you decided to come back."

Nikki's commitment to rumor, hearsay and scandal was the stuff of legend, and usually her information was as trustworthy as the World Almanac. But something was wrong with this picture.

"You know, Nikki, I think you have this one all wrong. Everybody knows that Alec can't be forced to do anything. And, anyway, the Baldwins didn't even know I was coming to the island."

"All I know is," the girl said with a crafty smile, "someone in legal said the client put it in the contract that you'd be on-site, and they wouldn't sign it if you didn't come. They were so determined, they said they'd find another firm to handle the job if Mr. Mackenzie couldn't get you to come back."

Daisy's head was pounding so relentlessly she was unable to take a moment to appreciate Virginia and Joseph's loyalty to her. A loyalty, she realized, that was far stronger and more resilient than Alec's own.

Her heart squeezed painfully and somehow it must have shown because Nikki leaned forward again and touched Daisy's cold hand. "I guess you got it worse than ever for him, don't you sweetie?"

Daisy didn't answer right away because her throat was threatening to seal up entirely. Clearly, everyone at Mackenzie Architectural knew that she'd been nursing a serious case of unrequited love for Alec. Soon they'd know just how blind that love had been. And then her humiliation would be complete.

Winning is what matters, Alec had said to her on the golf

course. *Winning* is what mattered to Alec Mackenzie. And boy, look what he'd been willing to do to win this time.

The memory of the electricity that had arced through her when he'd taken her hands in his and begged her to come back to work, of the earnestness on his handsome face when he told her how much he needed her. She knew now that when he'd told her he needed her, it had given her hope that he might someday feel more for her, something more like love. But he hadn't wanted her to come back to work at all. He'd just been lying to get what he really wanted: money, recognition, power, accolades…. Whatever it was, he'd lied to her and she'd believed every word.

The realization that everything else that had happened between her and Alec was also a lie settled over her like a cold mist. What a fool she'd been, she thought as her heart crumbled to dust. A stupid, hopeless, heartbroken fool.

Daisy tucked her hands beneath her to hide their trembling and pasted on a happy face for Nikki. "Oh, that," she said, rolling her eyes for effect. "I'm so over him." Then, in an effort to distract Nikki from giving her more details that she really didn't want to know, she added brightly, "Now, tell me all the news from the office," and settled in for a nice, long, one-sided conversation.

Eleven

Alec looked at his watch. Half past two. By now, Nosy Nikki would be back on the ferry and headed for home, so he locked up the construction trailer, jumped into his golf cart, pointed it toward the hotel and stepped on the accelerator. Hard.

He and Daisy had agreed that because of Nikki's eagle eye for scandal, he should make himself scarce this morning. She was sure to get a whiff of something juicy if she saw the hunger in his eyes when he looked at Daisy or if she heard how Daisy's voice dipped and softened when she spoke to him. So even though he'd hated to leave Daisy and their warm bed this morning, he'd departed early and gone to one of the job sites to hole up in the trailer and work on some drawings until it was time to go home.

He checked his watch again as he sped down the hill. He

had a vague sense that he was doing some pretty serious speeding because the other drivers—especially the ones he was passing—were giving him sour, disapproving looks. Too bad, he thought. He had somewhere to be.

Alec had no problem admitting that he was driving like a maniac because he was anxious to get home and spend the day with Daisy. The thing he was more reluctant to admit was that she'd gotten under his skin in a way no one ever had. He didn't know what that meant—hell, his heart had been buried so deep for so long, he wasn't even sure it could be resurrected, even by someone as amazing as Daisy—but he was pretty sure he was ready to get out the pickaxes and start digging.

And for Alec Mackenzie, that was pretty big talk.

He smiled to himself and whistled an off-key little ditty as he pulled to a stop outside their hotel. They'd talked about going hiking through the island's interior or renting a sailboat this afternoon. Of course, the way things had been going around here lately, he thought as he opened the front door, he wasn't sure they'd even make it out of the room. And that was just fine with him.

When he stepped inside the cool, quiet interior of their suite, the atmosphere seemed eerily calm. A strange, inexplicable chill hopped down his spine as he walked toward the bedrooms. At the last minute, a noise from Daisy's room made him turn left instead of right in his search.

"Daze?" he called out and reached down to scratch Bam Bam who was sitting outside Daisy's not-quite-closed door.

A loud thump came from inside her room so he moved one step closer and pushed open the door with a fingertip.

And that's when he saw her throwing things into her suitcase so fast you'd think the place was on fire.

He blinked. Twice. "What are you doing?" he asked, and stood still as a statue in the doorway even though his pulse had shifted into high gear.

She didn't even look up. "Packing."

"I can see that," he said, and swatted away a nagging sense of dread. "Where are you going?"

"Home." She pulled a stack of shirts from a drawer and savagely dumped them into her open bag.

Apprehension, sharp and insistent, trickled through him as he watched her whirling about the room in her haste. "I must have missed something. Why are you going home?"

"Because I can't stay here anymore."

He looked around the room, saw silk and lace spilling out of one drawer, sweaters falling out of another. One suitcase was already packed, a third sat empty at the foot of the bed. He searched for what could be wrong and came up empty.

"Daisy, what happened?"

"Section seven, paragraph D," she said matter-of-factly and handed him a thick sheaf of papers as she spun by him.

The Santa Margarita contract. It was opened to the section she'd mentioned. The heading read "Mackenzie Architectural Staffing Requirements."

So she knew. *Dammit.*

At first, it'd been a business decision not to tell her the circumstances that led to her being rehired. After all, he couldn't afford to have her refuse. Later, well, he knew he should have told her but honest to God, with everything they'd gone through in the last week, he'd just never found the right time.

"Hey," he said, taking a step toward her. "I know I should have told you but I thought you'd get upset." He tried a weak smile. "And look. I was right."

She shot him a look so deadly, it should have killed him where he stood.

"I'm sorry," he said, putting both hands up. "I am. I'm sorry I didn't tell you myself."

She zipped up the second suitcase and started packing the third. "Too little, too late," she said, repeating his words from the previous night. "You lied to me, Alec."

Anger rumbled deep in his gut but long practice kept it from marring his outward calm. "No. I said I wanted you to come back and I did."

"No, you didn't. You wanted to *win*. Well, congratulations," she said as she threw a pair of sneakers into the suitcase. "You won. You got what you wanted."

The pain in her eyes was so intense he had a sudden urge to take her into his arms and comfort her. But then, just as quickly, he swept the instinct aside.

"This isn't about winning and losing," he said, although he knew with a flash of unease that—originally, anyway—it had been about that very thing. "Oh, c'mon, Daze," he said, purposely trying to keep his voice even. "Don't be mad. You came back. I got the contract. We're a great team. Hasn't this all turned out for the best?"

"'I need you, Daisy,'" she quoted as if she hadn't heard him. "'I can't do this without you, Daisy.'" She stuffed a handful of bras into her suitcase. "Those are lies. And they're the basis for everything we've done together since."

She looked up at him, her expression aghast, her cheeks bright with embarrassment. "My God. This must be what it feels like to be one of your temporary bimbos," she said. "Poor girls," she muttered as she returned to her task with a shake of her dark, soft curls. "And to think I wasted so much time carrying a torch for you. Well, fortunately for me, I wised up before you could use me up and discard me."

The anger bubbled, then spilled into him, washing over him like a miserable, ruthless tide. "So you're leaving," he choked out. The heat in his voice scorched the very air around them.

"Yes. I'll explain to the Baldwins—"

"To hell with the Baldwins," he said, and turned away from her so she couldn't see the hurt he knew was showing in his eyes.

Of course she was leaving. *Of course.* Lord, he'd been out of his mind to believe she was different. What had he been thinking to let himself get so tangled up with her? For chrissakes, how could he have let himself get so close that she could hurt him at all?

When he heard her zipping up the last suitcase a moment later, he turned back to her, his face a carefully composed mask. When he spoke, he kept firm control over his voice, his expression, his body language. "I'll call accounting tomorrow morning and have them cut you a check."

She blinked and he watched, silent and grim, as the tears that had gathered in her dark, wounded eyes spilled over and slid down her cheeks.

And then Alec turned and walked away.

Because Alec hadn't had a relationship with his mother for so long, one of the many things he couldn't possibly have known about her was that she was as persistent as the moon pulling in the tides.

In the four days since Daisy had left, Barbara had called exactly four times, asking him to meet her for dinner. On

Thursday afternoon he finally relented and agreed to meet her the following night.

The longest day of the year was only few days away, so the sun was still clinging to the horizon as Alec walked to *The Galley* on Duncan Street to meet his mother for dinner.

He was in no hurry to get there. As he walked past the noisy, colorful, summer tourists swarming the pier, he noticed his steps were slow, his energy drained.

The last few days at work had been a disaster without Daisy, but the nights had been worse. Sleep had become nothing more than a dim, hazy memory as he lay alone in his big, empty bed night after night, thinking of how wonderful it had been to hold her, soft and sated, in his arms each night as he fell asleep. Thank God his days were full of the extra work her departure had left behind. It was the only time he wasn't completely preoccupied with thoughts of her and the heartbreaking look on her face when he'd last seen her.

He sighed and shoved his hands into the pockets of his jacket. It was for the best. He knew it was. But still, he couldn't deny that all the joy had leaked out of his life the minute he'd walked out the door. And now that Daisy was gone, it seemed that he was just putting one foot in front of the other in virtually every area of his life.

Thanks to her, work was now a lonely grind, the idea of shallow bimbos bored him silly, and waking up with a soft, warm woman—more specifically, Daisy Kincaid—in his arms had become as natural as breathing. Damn her, he thought. For worming her way into his life, into his mind and—it made him mad as hell to admit it—into his heart.

But what was he supposed to do? he thought crossly, when

by both word and deed, she'd made it clear she didn't want anything to do with him?

"Hello, Alec," his mother called out, waving at him from in front of the restaurant. "Hello!"

"Hi, Barbara," he said as he opened the door for her and accepted her continental, two-cheek air kiss in greeting.

"Was it a long walk?" she asked, then kept up a steady stream of nervous chatter as they were shown to their table.

Because they hadn't spoken in years, they had a lot to catch up on so they didn't lack for conversation during dinner. As the meal wound down, though, his mother grew quieter. After the coffee was served, she reached across the table, then stopped just short of touching his hand.

"Alec, I've been wanting to tell you something," she said as she pulled her hand back. "Something I should have told you a long time ago." She looked down into her cooling, untouched coffee and sucked in a big breath. "About three years before you were born, your father and I had another child. A son."

His hand tightened on his cup reflexively. "Are you telling me I have a—" But he stopped when she shook her head.

"No." Her voice was a whisper. He had to lean forward to hear what she said next. "Your brother died just three days before he would have been six months old."

Alec's throat constricted. It felt like someone was squeezing the air out of him little by little.

"Your father wanted to have another child right away but I couldn't do it." She looked up, and he saw her eyes were shiny with tears. "I was so afraid. No one could tell us why Christian had died, and I was sure I'd done something wrong…. God," she said quietly, "I loved that little boy so much."

For a moment the years-old grief was fresh in her eyes, and Alec could suddenly imagine her as a young woman, enduring the misery of losing her child. Just as suddenly, his heart began to ache for her.

"Anyway," she said as she dashed the tears away with the back of her hand, "of course, I finally got pregnant. With you." She smiled unsteadily. "You were such a wonderful little boy. So charming and sweet. But something had happened to me when we lost Christian. It was like I'd died, too. Inside," she said, and touched her heart with her fingertips.

She was silent for a moment, and while he stared into the eyes that were so much like his own, memories filled the silence. His mother and father fighting, the parade of nannies and housekeepers, the distance between himself and his parents that he'd always hoped to bridge, the way he'd tried so hard to win her attention, and how he'd finally given up hope.

"Essentially, Christian's death ended my marriage," she said finally. "But that wasn't the worst of it. The worst was what I did to you." Her deep-blue eyes burned with sorrow and regret. "Because I knew how much it would hurt to lose you, I refused to take the risk of loving you." She reached out then and took his hand, gripped it hard. "Of course," she said, and he heard her voice crackle with long-pent-up emotion, "in the end it wasn't something I could control. I loved you, anyway." She squeezed his hand again. "How could I not?" she asked with a pale smile. "You were my baby."

He smiled, too, and had to make an effort to quell the emotional tsunami raging inside him. "I know," he said simply, and tightened his own hold on her fingers.

"I'm sorry, Alec. I missed out on so much."

"It's all right," he said, surprised that he really meant it. "I'm glad you told me. It explains so much."

She cleared her throat awkwardly, her smile growing. "There's one more thing."

"There's more?" he asked and his mother laughed.

"I want to start over, Alec. Let's face it, I have more days behind me than I do in front of me—"

He must have looked alarmed because she stopped short and said, "No, no. Everything's fine. I just don't want to waste anymore time. And someday you'll give me grandchildren—"

"Don't count on it," he interrupted, but his words lacked some of the conviction they would have had a week or two earlier.

She didn't pry, she just stirred her cold coffee and let it go. "You're a good man, Alec," she said with just a shadow of sadness. "You did a good job raising yourself."

He smiled. "Not everyone would agree with you, Mom," he said. "But thanks."

And after they'd finished their coffee and had made plans to get together the following week, he walked home through the bustling center of town and thought about how she'd chosen not to be a mother to keep herself safe from being hurt. He thought about how she'd run away and hidden behind her work. And then he thought about how badly that had backfired for everyone.

But it wasn't until much, much later when the pinkening dawn was peering through the shutters and he was still staring up at the ceiling that he realized how much he and his mother were alike. She'd tried to shield herself from love, and all she'd really done was grow older, isolated and lonely and filled with regrets. He'd done the same, tried to keep himself from falling in love with Daisy, and now here he was, miserable and alone.

Alec knew that Daisy had probably already slipped beyond his reach. He'd been a jerk—and not just during their last conversation. He'd been a jerk to Daisy almost since he'd met her. He'd taken her for granted on a daily basis, been too busy selfishly protecting himself to see that she truly cared for him. Because of that, he'd thrown an endless parade of inferior women in her face. And then, to reward her for her loyalty, he'd used her to secure this job and his professional reputation.

For three long years Daisy had given him everything. Even, apparently, her love. And he'd given her nothing but a paycheck.

Now that he understood that, he wondered why it had taken her so long to quit.

Alec looked out the window and saw the sky lighten, watched the subtle pinks and blues blend and dance as he waited impatiently for the world to come awake.

As soon as it did, he was going to go to L.A. and do whatever it took to find Daisy and get her back. Only this time he'd ditch the lies and deceit. This time he was going to tell the truth.

Hopefully, he wasn't too late. Because he had no intention of growing old bitter and alone. He was going to grow old happy and fulfilled and peaceful.

With Daisy.

Daisy sat on the porch with Bam Bam stretched bonelessly across her lap and looked out over the lovely, crystalline blue Pacific and the lush, intricately tended gardens that surrounded the Baldwins' guest cottage. The early-morning sky was painted in magnificent shades of pastel, and the distant shores of Los Angeles were muted and softened by a misty fog.

For the sixth day in a row, she'd woken up in paradise, she thought as she ran a hand absently over the cat's soft fur. But the grand display that nature had been putting on was wasted on her because Daisy had never been so unhappy in all her life.

A week ago, when she'd come to offer both her thanks and her apologies to the Baldwins, she'd had every intention of getting on the next ferry back to Los Angeles and starting the long process of getting on with her life. It was Virginia who'd suggested that she take a week to relax and reflect before making any decisions about the future. Daisy had been reluctant, but eventually she'd accepted their generous offer of the lovely little cottage tucked far up the hill behind the main house.

The week had been tranquil, peaceful and terribly, terribly lonely.

Even though her last image of Alec was that of his angry, frozen eyes just before he walked out of her life, the memories that had been haunting both her waking hours and her restless nights were far more disturbing: his blue eyes shifting to a dark azure just before he'd taken her in his arms that first rainy day; his twinkling eyes filled with laughter as he'd watched her making sand angels on the beach; the stunned look on his face when she'd walloped him at chess; the tender spark she'd seen in his gaze when she'd first explored his body with her hands and her mouth.

A shiver of pure longing passed through her, and she felt deeply sad. It was time. Time to go home and begin again.

She spent the morning packing, then walked down to the main house to say goodbye. Virginia had been a gracious hostess and a patient friend from the first, listening to Daisy's tearful explanation of what had happened without making judgments or blaming either Alec or Daisy. Now she hugged Daisy and told her to call anytime she needed a shoulder, to come back anytime she needed refuge.

By noon Daisy had returned her cart to the Hotel Margarita and was waiting at the ferry landing for the next boat.

She dropped down onto her largest suitcase and set Bam Bam's cage by her feet. It was Saturday and the harbor was thronging with tourists, newly arrived and full of energy. Herds of Scouts and school kids crowded the dock, pushing and shoving and laughing as they sorted through the mountains of gear they'd brought. Teenagers flew by on their skateboards, parents chased after their children and couples strolled hand in hand along the boardwalk.

Daisy sighed, overwhelmed by the twists and turns of the past few weeks. She didn't know how she was going to do it, but she was going to stop loving Alec Mackenzie. And she was going to start by picking up the pieces of her heart and gluing them back together with whatever optimism she could dredge up from the bottom of her own personal well. And she would start immediately, if not sooner.

"I've been looking everywhere for you," a deep, profoundly familiar voice said from behind her.

She twisted around, her pulse jumping and skittering. Alec wore a rumpled denim shirt and khakis that needed pressing and he hadn't gotten close enough to a razor to make a difference in days. He looked, as usual, gorgeous. He smiled at her, his eyes crinkling up at the corners, and her heart betrayed her and picked up the pace. He'd lied to her, he'd used her and he'd left her and her body didn't care.

Lied, used, left, she repeated to herself and clung to it like a life preserver. *Lied, used, left.*

"Why? Did you forget to say something?" she asked, holding her resolve in place by the sheer force of her will and her remembered anger.

"As a matter of fact, I did," he said as he hunkered down in front of her. He searched her face, settled on her eyes. "My God, I've missed you, Daze."

She wanted to look away but couldn't. She was stuck, like filings on a magnet. "That's what you forgot to say?"

She clutched her bag in front of her, saw the ferry approaching out of the corner of her eye. *Thank goodness.* In minutes she'd be able to make her escape.

"No, I forgot one other thing."

She waited. Whatever he said wasn't going to make a difference. She was leaving, any minute now. Soon she'd be safe from his lies, his thoughtless, selfish manipulations, his—

"I love you, Daisy."

She dropped her bag, heard her stuff spill out onto the dock. She started to bend over to retrieve it, but the action brought her too close to him so she pulled back. Vaguely, she heard the people around them begin to whisper and murmur in curiosity as Alec scooped everything back into her bag and righted it.

The wattage of his smile burned into her. Heat flushed her cheeks. "Did you hear me?"

"No," she said. "I'm sure I didn't. It sounded like you said—"

"I love you," he repeated, his smile wide and sincere.

She didn't believe him. She couldn't. She'd be the

biggest fool in ten counties if she let him hurt her again. Lord, how she wanted to believe him. But how could she, when she already knew how far he'd go to get what he wanted?

Her heart was pounding so fast she felt breathless. "I have to go, Alec. So just tell me why you're really here." She willed the ferry to hurry. Please hurry, she begged silently. *If I don't run soon, I'm going to get caught loving him again.*

Alec didn't blame her for doubting him. The way he'd jerked her around for the past three years, it was no wonder she was looking at him like he was speaking Swahili. Hell, he'd only figured the whole damn thing out about seven hours ago himself.

He drank her in, like a thirsty man falling upon an oasis. She looked beautiful but sad, like a wounded angel trying to take flight. Her brown eyes were huge and wary, her smooth cheeks were stained by emotion, her full, lush lips were tight and tense. He wanted to kiss it all away, make everything okay. But that wasn't enough. He owed her more.

He touched his shirt pocket for the dozenth time in an hour. He'd already been to L.A. and back by helicopter, visited her house and found her youngest brother, Sean, bringing in the mail. Now that he'd met one of her trio of bodyguards, he understood her complaint about being watched over too closely. It had taken quite some time to explain everything to the suspicious, fiercely protective man, but eventually Alec's earnestness had won the day. Sean had given up her whereabouts and wished Alec luck as he ran back to his waiting cab.

Now that he was here, Alec didn't know what to say first, there was so much he needed to get out. And, he thought as he glanced at the approaching ferry, he had to make it snappy.

"I'm so damned sorry I wasn't straight with you, Daze. I

know I've made a mess of everything." He shook his head and it felt leaden, heavy with regret for what an ass he'd been.

"I was a big, dumb, blind fool. And you were right here all along, hiding in plain sight." He saw her checking the ferry's progress and knew his time was running out. "I was so busy pushing people away, I couldn't see that you were the one person—the only person—I've ever wanted to hold close to me." He touched his chest, right over his heart, then pulled his hand away to rake his fingers through his hair.

"I just didn't get it before. But once you were gone and the whole world faded to black-and-white, I figured it out quick."

She was still silent but at least she was listening. Her hands were clasped tightly in her lap, and when he reached out and pulled her left hand into his, he could feel her pulse beneath his fingers, quick and restless.

"Daisy, I love you," he said. "I do." His hand shook as he pulled the black velvet box out of his shirt pocket but he didn't care. "I don't deserve it but please believe me just one more time. I want you. I need you. I can't do this without you." He flipped the box open with his thumb. "Please marry me and make me an honest man."

Alec sensed more than saw the crowd that had gathered around them as the flawless three-carat solitaire glinted in the bright, island sun, casting a million tiny prisms all around them. It was perfect, this public demonstration to atone for his very private sins.

Daisy's gaze was fixed on his eyes as if she were searching for an answer there. He smiled, nodded, encouraged her to keep looking because he knew his whole heart was shining in his eyes. It's all right there, he told her silently. *It's all right there.*

He saw the smile play about her lips first, then watched it spread to her eyes where it burned off the wariness little by little. "You want to marry me."

He nodded as relief began to seep into his body. "More than I've ever wanted anything in my whole sad, sorry life," he said.

She glanced down at the ring, then her gaze shot back up to his and she bit into her bottom lip.

"And you're really Alec Mackenzie? This isn't an *Invasion of the Body Snatchers* thing?"

He chuckled. "Nope. One hundred percent, authentic, homegrown me."

She suppressed a grin. "I'm still going to open my bed-and-breakfast," she said. "And I won't let you win at golf."

His lips twitched into a brief smile, then he nodded solemnly. "I know," he said. "Those are just two of the reasons I love you."

She grinned, bright and quick, but it faded just as fast. She lowered her voice so all the interested passersby couldn't hear. "Do you really think you can do it, Alec? Become a one-woman man?

"It's too late for that, sweetheart. I already am," he said, and his heart hammered hard as he slipped the ring onto her finger and pulled her to her feet. "Now say you'll marry me."

She looked at the ring again, cocked her head to the side, then looked up and held his gaze for a long, suspended moment. Then she pulled her hands from his, slipped them up and over his shoulders and tipped his forehead down to hers.

They were both trembling, both intensely aware of the scrutiny of the lingering, expectant onlookers, and yet he knew with a humbling certainty that he would have gladly stood there for an eternity just to keep her sweet little body pressed up against his.

"Yes," she whispered. "I will."

To Alec it seemed the world around them let out a long-held breath and began to stir, revolving around them in a swirl of color and energy. He dragged her into his arms, kissed her deeply and hungrily.

The ferry's horn blew, loud and insistent, and Alec pulled away, just an inch, but it seemed like miles. "Tell me," he said. "Tell me you love me like I love you. A forever, damn-the-torpedoes, bolt-the-doors-and-make-wild-passionate-love-for-a-hundred-years kind of love."

She smiled up at him. "It's exactly that kind of love, you idiot. It always has been." And with that she pulled him down to her, kissed him fiercely and sweetly and eternally.

She finally came up for air as the passengers bound for the mainland began to flow around them. "Would you look at what I just did?" she asked, shooting him a wicked grin as she crowded her body up against his and set him on fire. "I got within your arm's length."

And even though the world around them had always been cast in every color of the rainbow, Alec realized that he was seeing everything in vivid Technicolor for the very first time in his life.

He pulled her closer, lowered his head to hers and breathed against her soft lips, "I thought you'd never get here, sweetheart. I thought you'd never get here."

* * * * *

is thrilled to bring you

Three brand-new books in

Alexandra Sellers's
popular miniseries

Powerful sheikhs born
to rule and destined
to find their
princess brides…

SONS
OF THE
DESERT

Be sure to look for…

SHEIKH'S CASTAWAY
#1618 November 2004

THE ICE MAIDEN'S SHEIKH
#1623 December 2004

THE FIERCE AND TENDER SHEIKH
#1629 January 2005

Available at your favorite retail outlet.

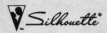